BOOK WRITTEN BY

J T FISHER

OKAY, SO I LIED!

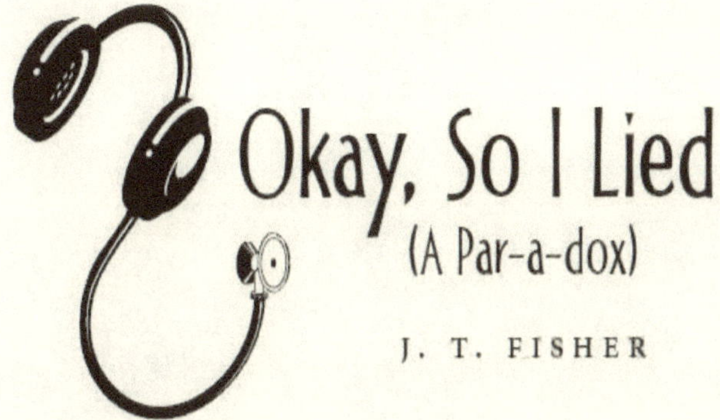

Okay, So I Lied
(A Par-a-dox)

J. T. FISHER

ISBN: 978-1-961677-66-1 (Paperback)

Library of Congress Control Number: 2025919989

Printed in the United States of America

Published by

info@thequippyquill.com
(302) 295-2278

CONTENTS

Chapter 1 1

Chapter 2 11

Chapter 3 25

Chapter 4 33

Chapter 5 39

Chapter 6 47

Chapter 7 65

Chapter 8 77

Chapter 9 91

Chapter 10 109

Chapter 11 125

Chapter 12 135

Chapter 13 147

Chapter 14 163

Chapter 15 177

Chapter 16 193

Chapter 17 207

Chapter 18 219

Chapter 19 233

Chapter 20 247

Chapter 21 259

Life begins when you put your fantasies to rest
and make your dreams come true…

--- Doug Kipnis

Chapter 1

Damn it! This day is going to last forever. Jill Kelly had been plotting and planning this all weekend, and she was now slogging through the last few hours until the moment when she would have to come clean. She lay sprawled across her childhood bed while the light patterns danced on the ceiling. Somehow, it didn't matter if it was morning or afternoon. They were always there.

The scientific side of her mind would have her think that it was because the house was situated in such way that her bedroom faced the southeast. Channeling her father, her mind went into methodical calculations of angles and numbers to figure what time it was. She rolled over and looked over at the alarm clock on her nightstand.

Jill's emotional mind could only see the flashes of light, sending her into her daydreams of becoming that music star she had always dreamed of being… standing on the edge a stage, rocking out to her latest hit in front of thousands.

On this particular day though, a typical Sunday in the Kelly household, she was lying there alone while her brother Ivan was away at Duke University, probably either looking to get laid or playing baseball. Her brother Eric, home this weekend from the University of Pennsylvania, was likely at the library studying. Jill was next to leave for college. Her father, Arnie, was in the back bedroom sprawled out on the bed watching college basketball, and her mom, Doris was either in the kitchen baking something or in the utility room folding laundry. It was unusual to have her father around. He had been traveling so much lately, to all those conferences and seminars, delivering remarks about his new heart procedure. She was just glad he was home this particular weekend.

What a mundane life she had been leading. Jill tried as hard as she could to fall asleep rather than succumb to the anxiety she was feeling about having "that conversation" at dinner that night. She had mulled it over in her mind, and had tried as hard as she could to come up with a strong argument, but she was absolutely certain she knew what her father's reaction to her proposal would be. In fact, she knew, almost verbatim, what he would say.

Her mind raced back to when she was little, perched on the piano bench next to her "Daddio," as she used to call him, singing for hours together. They would cover an entire Broadway Show score, with Arnie singing all the male parts and Jill doing all of the female roles. He would giggle at her attempting to reach the high notes for the songs meant for sopranos, like when she tried to sing "Climb Every Mountain." He finally suggested that she sing it an octave lower, and then she would proceed to knock his socks off with her natural given talent.

Together they participated in the church choir and performed in all of the holiday pageants. Arnie constantly displayed her talent at his medical office Christmas parties and when company came over, and they would sing duets of some of their favorite folk and groups; "Peter Paul and Mary," "Simon and Garfunkel," and even a little "Bob Dylan." That was one album he had from that group, "Paradox Lost." Then there was that one song, "Let your Heart Be Free." Daddio always got quiet when they did that song. Jill never knew why, and she never got up the nerve to ask him.

Arnie's favorite thing to do, though, was to get her to sing some of Streisand's early songs, like "Second Hand Rose," or "Sam, You Made the Pants Too Long," after dressing her up in either his or her mother's clothes. Ah, Jill reflected, those were the good old days.

When she started high school, though, "Daddio" became just Dad. He had suddenly taken on a whole new persona. He didn't seem to have time to sit at the piano, with all his traveling, but mainly because he thought she should be studying and buckling down at school. There was much less participation at the church, and the only show she could recall was when he cajoled her into auditioning for the role of "Peter Pan." She was still so slight then, even at fifteen, so she could pull it off, and yet she could belt out a song that would rattle the windows.

Jill was intelligent. School always came very easy to her. She barely picked up a book and was able to regurgitate information that it took other students' hours of intense study to learn. She could read and write at three and a half years old, and especially excelled in science and math. She knew that Arnie had always wanted her to follow in his footsteps and become a doctor. All of the men in the Kelly family had always been doctors, all the way back to her great-grandfather.

Mom just wanted her to be happy, but never really said as much. At least, that's what Jill was led to believe. Mom never really said much at all when Dad was talking. She never defended her. Whatever he said seemed to be the law of the land when it came to the rules of the house; where they went on vacations; what kind of car to buy; how to punish the kids when they did wrong… everything. Doris was, in essence, Arnie's shadow when he was around.

When he was away at a Cardiology Convention or on camping trip with his college cronies, Arnie's influence on Doris was minimized, and like a turtle, she would peek out from under her shell and offer herself to Jill. It was during those times when they could bond, openly and honestly. Doris had a modest understanding of Jill's plight, but having never had any self-directed hobbies or interests of her own, she didn't have the nerve to stand up to Arnie. Jill had to rely solely on her own ability and self-confidence, with the exception of the support of her brother Eric, who was at least able to empathize with her. Eric never felt like he was good enough for his father because he wasn't a jock on top of being a brilliant student.

Clouds must have blocked the sun as there were no more dancing lights on her ceiling. Jill closed her eyes and tried to imagine the dinner table that night. Mom had been planning a big meal. Dad did have his favorites: veal parmesan, pasta, garlic rolls and a Caesar salad. Eric would be late to the table because he had to "just finish this chapter," and the conversation would first be the day's basketball scores. Eric liked basketball. Liked it, but that was all. Arnie got more enthusiasm from the garlic roll when it slipped out of his hand, rolled off the table and hit the floor.

"Okay, then, Eric. What were you studying before dinner?" Arnie wasn't being sarcastic or angry, although Eric did not share his love for sports. Eric was a bookworm. He had to work a lot harder in school than Jill, especially when he was getting ready for midterms.

Eric was a bio-chemistry major, and planned to study medicine. He was going to go into Cardiology and join his father in his practice.

It was Ivan, the older son that shared Arnie's enthusiasm for the basketball. Ivan's sports ability and his athletic scholarship were the only things that would get him through school though because he would never make it on brains. Ivan would never become a doctor. The whole family came to terms with that a long time ago. Jill had even overheard her father one night, praying that his oldest son would make it as a professional athlete, or at least find a way to earn a living in the sports industry.

Jill, like Eric, was not an athlete, but took remarkable care of her body. She was small and slim. She ran distance although, not for her school team, but for her own meditation and wellbeing. She followed just enough of NCAA basketball to participate in the dinner conversation a little bit. On this particular night for Jill, however, it was only to stall the inevitable.

"It was the last part of a section from my Microbiology textbook." Eric was trying to get his knife through a piece of gristle when the knife slipped, and now his garlic roll went flying. "Maybe someone is trying to tell us something?" Eric said as he leaned over to pick it up from the floor.

Arnie laughed and turned to his daughter. Jill was not very attractive or popular, and suffered socially as a result. She had a few close friends, mostly from her music classes and the drama club, and her brother Eric. Eric got her. Thank God for Eric. He was going to be a doctor, and by so doing, perhaps save her from the same fate.

"Your turn," Arnie said.

Jill had been so focused on how she thought the conversation would or should go at dinner, that when her father put the spotlight on her, she was frozen. "What do you mean, my turn?"

Arnie simply picked up the garlic roll and waved it in front of him.

Relieved, Jill picked hers up, and promptly took a big bite. She still didn't know how she was going to begin the conversation that she needed to have. She made eye contact with Eric, who was sitting directly across from her. He kicked her gently under the table and nodded. Jill knew he was with her and would try his best to support her.

But this wasn't her Daddio; this was Dr. Kelly to whom she was going to try to talk. Maybe it wasn't dinner conversation after all.

Eric kicked her again. Jill glanced over and saw that her father had nearly cleared his plate. One thing she knew was that it's always better to have difficult conversations with him on a full stomach, because he would be much more likely to be relaxed and open-minded, than if he was hungry or tired.

"Um, Dad?" Jill could feel her dinner sitting heavily. The last bite of the garlic roll seemed to be pressing against her vocal chords, not a particularly strong attribute for someone about to try to make a case for studying voice and music theory as a college major. She delicately cleared her throat.

"Dad." She was prepared for this. She had mapped out her strategy all afternoon. She reached behind her a carefully picked up a folder that she had placed on the credenza earlier that afternoon, which housed a good portion of her armament. Arnie was still.

"This is my college application folder." She paused. Doris put her fork down. Eric gave her a reassuring glance. "I've actually heard from all of the schools to which I applied."

"All of them? Even UNC?" Arnie sat up in his chair.

The folder in Jill's hand began to rattle as her whole body trembled. Here it was. "Daddy, I didn't apply to UNC."

"What? Why not?" Shocked, a deep furrow began to form between his eyes. His lips parted, readying to speak further, but no words would come out. Before he could manage his thoughts, Jill began to make clear her carefully planned strategy.

"I've been doing a great deal of thinking and soul searching, Dad," turning her head to the other end of the table, "Mom." Wobbling, she sat back in the chair, placed the folder next to her plate, and proceeded to explain herself. Her neck was beginning to throb.

Having done extensive research before she ever even submitted the first college application, Jill had applied to several schools that specialize only in music, including Oberlin College in Ohio, and Berklee College of Music in Massachusetts. She also had completed applications to Stanford, Michigan, the University of Pennsylvania and Indiana University.

"I've decided that I don't necessarily want to go to medical school." There. She said it. The weight she had been carrying floated up and hung in the air. Jill half expected it to come crashing down on her head, so she looked directly at Eric for moral support. He wasn't there. He was focused on his father.

"And what is it you plan to study and then do with your life?" Arnie sat back in his chair, sporting a knowing smirk. His daughter thought she was dropping a bomb, but had alluded to this before, so he looked to her like he was ready.

"I want to study music. I want to sing. And act." *Why were there ants crawling under my skin?* Jill had never felt more uncomfortable in her life.

"Well," began Artie. He already had his response prepared. Arnie had his own research.

He did. He knew this was coming. Did Mom blow my cover? Did Eric?

While Jill was convinced, he would explode into a tirade, he seemed to lay before her a well-thought-out explanation as to why she shouldn't make this decision. He was even prepared with statistics. There were numbers about how many kids play high school basketball and never make it to the NBA, how many kids major in music and never sell a recording or book a concert, about how many years it took the top one hundred Oscar and Emmy winning actors to get their first roles other than television commercials.

Arnie presented numbers on the average hours of rehearsal time, how much it costs for road trips and going rates for paying the musicians. He seemed to know exactly everything there was to know. He was definitely ready for this argument. He talked about the lousy joints she would have to play and how impossible it would be to get an agent or a recording contract. He went on for ten minutes, and with each passing moment, Jill could almost feel the blood traveling from throughout her body, up the back of her neck to her brain. By the time he had put his papers down, Jill was in tears, her head pounding.

"Dad." Jill was going for the heart now.

"Have you no faith in me? In my talent or my ability to persevere?" She wiped a tear from her cheek, seeing a nod from Eric out of the corner of her eye.

Doris had been silent until now. "Honey, of course we know you're talented," she mumbled.

As usual, Arnie interrupted. "That's not the point." He went on. "You are going to have to support yourself until you succeed. What are you going to do? Wait on tables? Park cars? Work as a check-out girl in the grocery store?" His voice had been growing to a crescendo. It seemed as though he was coming in for the kill as if it were time to end this. Arnie had enough aggravation with Ivan, although his oldest son had gifts other than academic ones. At least he was trying. Jill knew her father respected her intelligence and abilities in math and science. Music was just for fun.

"This is my last word on this." Arnie stood up, picked his paperwork and turned directly toward his daughter. "If you choose to major in music or drama, I will not be contributing to your college education. You will have to find a way to pay for it yourself." He paused. "Tread lightly here, my dear. I'm saying this because I know of what I speak."

Arnie turned on his heels, headed down the hallway, calling back over his shoulder, "I only want the best for you. A few years of medical school, a couple of internships and a residency, and you'll have a life beyond your wildest dreams." He stopped before he turned the corner into the den. "Help your mother with the dishes."

Grudgingly, Jill gathered her papers. She was NOT going to let her father smash her fantasies. She couldn't understand why he was so adamant about this. He had always encouraged her when it came to music and acting. *What did he mean by that? So much antagonism? I know of what I speak... BULLSHIT. He's not going to ruin my life and my dreams.*

She stood up, still lost in reflection. She would have to rethink things. Maybe she would attend the University of Pennsylvania, or Michigan.

I know somebody famous went there. Then there was Indiana University which had the Jacobs School of Music (considered to be one of the best in the country). All of this ran through her head as she cleared the table. Her legs still felt like rubber, her heart still pounding. *It didn't go well, but at least I got conversation started,* she thought. *And why the hell is he so dead set against this? We used to have so much fun singing together. The show tunes... the old torch songs. Even that old obscure folk rock group he always listened to, that one album by Paradox Lost.*

Although her parents knew nothing about it, during her ninth and tenth grade years, Jill had taken voice lessons from a professional opera singer. Last year, she worked intensely with a different teacher who taught her more pop techniques. For all of her high school years, they thought she was a member of the Future Doctor's Club, and that her afternoons were being spent at club meetings, visiting the children's hospital and volunteering at various nursing homes in the area. It had been difficult for her to keep up this deception. It made her feel so guilty lying all of the time. Only Eric knew.

She would eventually have to double back and come clean about all of this, and she wasn't quite sure when and how to do it. She couldn't stand all of this sneakiness and lying, but would soon discover that this was only the beginning of many deceptions she would be compelled to perpetrate.

"You don't own me. It's my life. You can't tell me what to do. I'm an adult. Don't tell me what to study..."

Jill's mind was overtaken and she thought back to an old song her old Daddio used to play for her to sing when she was younger... she stared at the dark ceiling in her bedroom and drifted off to sleep.

"You don't own me. I'm gonna get there one way or another, Daddio

Chapter 2

Jill scampered across the Indiana University campus to the registrar's office, already late for her 10:00 am appointment with the curriculum counselor. While she knew her parents were not manipulative or maniacal, as she had seen with some of her friends, there was still an ounce of worry in her that her father may have interceded with a phone call. It took everything she had in her to convince him that IU was a good undergraduate program for premed, and that she promised to at least apply to his alma mater, UNC Chapel Hill, for medical school. It was a difficult trip up to Indiana. Jill was just glad they had to get back to Charlotte last night to see to her Dad's surgery schedule this morning and her mom's bridge game this afternoon.

While she didn't like lying, Jill couldn't see another way of paying for school. Not being honest with her parents had always been a source of anxiety for her. That coupled with the fact that her Dad had sworn up and down a thousand times that he would NEVER pay for her to study voice and acting had already taken a toll on her. It weighed heavily on her that she didn't understand the genesis of his resolve. Her Daddio had always been her best music partner and friend. Nobody else in the house understood her love for music. But then it abruptly ended.

Jill reached the Old Crescent, near Dunn Wood. Out of breath, she tripped up the few Indiana limestone steps into Franklin Hall. She, like most freshman, looked lost. She felt a tap on her shoulder, and as she spun around, her backpack knocked into the arm of a tall, skinny, but handsome young man. "Can I help you find something?"

"I need to change my classes before next week," she started. She wasn't sure if she was even in the right place to do that, but it was at least a start. "I have an appointment with a career counselor, who I think is in this building." She blushed, a little. "I haven't even started yet and I'm changing my major."

"Join the club." Mike was at IU originally to study some kind of science, and had already put in a year completing the basic undergraduate work, but like his brother before him, he was, at his very core, a musician. He was studying saxophone and jazz history. "My name is Michael. And you are?"

"Oh, I'm sorry. I'm Jill." Already late, Jill didn't want to stand around and talk, so she asked for directions to the career office. With a quick thank you, she was off toward the elevator. When she turned back again, Michael was gone. She beat herself up about being so rude. *It would have been nice to have made a friend on her first day.* Shrugging her shoulders, she entered the elevator and pushed the button. As no one else was with her, she took the opportunity to rehearse the canned dialogue that she had planned to use on the counselor about switching her major. One thing she needed to find out about was how semester grades were reported. She didn't want any 'snail' mail delivered to her address in Charlotte, North Carolina. In fact, she had already decided that going home next summer wasn't even an option. It would be hard enough to get through Thanksgiving, winter break and spring break.

When the elevator doors opened, she was fully prepared for the next step in the process. She looked to the left and then to the right. There were no signs in the hallway and no numbers on the doors. What was worse, there was nobody around from whom to get some direction. Her legs started to feel that familiar antsy feeling as the elevator doors closed behind her. Although she had always had a problem with anxiety and fear, stage fright had never been a problem. She was going to act "as if." This was how she intended to get through even the toughest times. It was how she landed in Bloomington, Indiana to begin with.

She started down the hallway to her right and knocked on the first door she saw. When she heard nothing, she moved on to the next.   Relieved when she heard the words "Come in," she confidently opened the solid oak door to reveal what appeared to be a waiting room, each chair filled. The front desk had a small sign on it that read, "Pardon our Dust as we remodel." That, she figured, is why there were no signs or numbers anywhere.

"Is this the career counseling center?"

"Take a number and have a seat." The voice from behind the window sounded irritated. Likely a student who didn't care to be up that early on a Monday morning, he added, "Unless you have an appointment. Then, sign in on the pad over there." All Jill could see was a hand with a finger pointing to her left. She signed her name and the time of her appointment and sat down, dropping her backpack beside her. She wiggled her phone out of the back of her pocket to check if she had gotten any messages or emails, and saw that she was only a few minutes late after all. No messages, no calls, no emails, she shoved it into her backpack, sat back and glanced around the room.

After ten minutes of waiting, and assessing the other students waiting, a trait she had picked up from her father, Jill got up to ask what was holding up her appointment. She learned her judging from her father and her impatience from her mother. The mystery man behind the window finally revealed his face. He took a long sip from his oversized coffee cup and explained that her counselor was running a few minutes late, but she could fill out some forms in the meantime.

Jill took the clipboard, returned to her seat, and began to answer questions that would eventually change the course of not only her college career but her entire life. Name: *well that one was easy enough*. Date of birth: *got it*. Student identification number: *did they mean social security number or is there an actual student ID number? First dumb question. Not going up to ask.* Local address: *Remember that*. Telephone: *Easy one*. Current Class: *Freshman*. Current Declared Major: *Biology*.

"Kelly, Jill" came a voice from the side door next to the welcome desk. When Jill looked up, she swore she saw George Clooney standing in the doorway beyond the window, holding a manila folder. After a suspended double-take, she raised her hand, leaned over and grabbed her backpack, causing the clipboard to slide off of her lap to the floor. When she leaned over to pick that up, her backpack slipped off of her shoulder and knocked the clipboard out of her hand and it shimmied across the linoleum floor, sliding to a stop at George's feet. He bent over to pick it up, giving Jill time to gather herself and her things and sheepishly walk over to him. As she neared, she realized, obviously, that he was not George Clooney, but Carl Nixon, a career counselor, and nothing more. His name tag was crystal clear on that. She took a deep breath, and began to act "as if."

"Sorry about that. I'm Jelly. Uh, I mean Jill Kelly" She blushed, feeling as if she had already destroyed her chances of being accepted into this premiere program, but he motioned her through the door, and then to follow him. As they entered his 'office,' which was no bigger than a cubicle with a door, he handed the clipboard back to her and with the same motion, pointed to a chair. At that moment, Jill figured she would have to do most of the talking. After her entrance, she wasn't sure she could handle it.

"Why are you here today?" George didn't leave much room for pleasantries. She meant Carl. She had to get that first impression out of her head. "It said on your form that you are pretty much set to start classes next week."

"Mr. Nixon..." Jill started tentatively. She didn't know if transferring from regular Indiana University to the Jacobs School of Music was handled here or if it wasn't done until junior year or what. "I don't want to major in Biology."

The counselor sat back at his small desk, in his worn chair. "You can change major anytime. You still need to do the lower college requirements." Carl Nixon was tired and pretty much over whiny college students.

He had been doing this for thirty-two years and close to retiring. "What did you want to switch to? Something else in the sciences?"

Jill already didn't like his attitude. "Actually, I want to major in voice and music theory. I really wanted to know if I needed to transfer over to the Jacobs School now or after I finish the Associates Degree requirements." Jill tried to sound knowledgeable, as if she had done her research, but she had only found that this was the best school she could attend that wasn't ONLY a music school.

Carl sat up in his chair. "First of all, you can't just transfer to Jacobs. But if you want music, this is where you want to be." Something awakened in him. "What kind of music do you like? I mean, what area do you intend to study? Do you sing? Play an instrument? What?" It was as if he was a different person. Was he already her biggest fan?

"You can't just be transferred into Jacobs; you have to audition to get in. You'll have to start where you are and send in your audition tape. Let me check what the deadline is for the next semester." Carl was almost frantic. He was clicking, typing, clicking, and typing madly on his computer.

Jill finally spoke. "Whoa. Mr. Nixon, slow down." She wondered what it was that created this frenzy. Perhaps he was a musician himself. Maybe it was a fantasy of his.

"Okay, you have about ten weeks to get a tape to them for the January semester admittance. It really helps that you are already here, studying. We can't switch colleges until you get accepted to

Jacobs, just your major." He was almost disappointed. "Just stick with what you have unless you want to change an elective. You can take a music class there as a non-music major if it's an elective." Carl was confident that he had found a temporary solution. "Let's do that. What do you want to take? A Voice class? It has to be an intro class or a seminar."

Jill decided, during the mad-typist session, that she was willing to do whatever it took to make this happen. "That would be great." She scanned the list of classes given at Jacobs that fit both her agenda and her schedule. She didn't even know where the school was located in relation to her dorm or her other classes. That didn't matter. Somehow, someway, she would make that one class her priority. "Is there a way I can take a class that is also a requirement in the School of Music curriculum, like Intro to Music Theory?"

"Yes, you can take that. That's both an Intro course and taught as a seminar."

"Great, is there space in the Tuesday Thursday evening seminar?" Jill figured and evening class was best because it wasn't conflicting with anything. It would fulfill a requirement once she gets accepted, and it was something that would serve as a crumpled ray of hope for her future." As Carl filled out the forms on his computer, Jill's mind took her a million miles away. She envisioned the lights on the ceiling of her bedroom in North Carolina morphing into that soundstage in her future. There were no more antsy feelings in her legs, yet her heart was pounding in her chest.

"Okay, done!" George sat back in his chair. Jill had to shake her head. *His name is not George. It's Carl.* "When you get a chance, you can go to the Jacobs website and find out all the specifics about the audition requirements. They'll want a specific piece… I think it's **Star Vicino**… and make sure you do it in the best key so you don't challenge yourself too much…" Carl scribbled the name of the piece on a scrap of paper. "Just double check that they haven't changed this."

When the schedule change was completed, Jill jumped up, secure in her actions, and then confidently picked up the strap of her backpack. She swung it over her shoulder and across her back. Carl handed her a printed copy of her new schedule, the scrap of paper that held the key to her future, and then his hand, offered in congratulations. She couldn't get over the change in his demeanor during the brief time she had spent with him. She boldly extended her hand in return. She did, indeed, have her first fan.

"Thank you, Mr. Nixon. I appreciate your help." Jill had accomplished the first step in her transition from doctor to rock star. Turning around in the tight space between her chair and the door, it dawned on her that she not only had reached the launching pad, but she had just added some fuel. As she closed the door behind her, it made her think one of her favorite Elton John songs, and almost skipped through the waiting room singing, "I'm not the person they think I am at home, Oh, no... baby... I'm launching myself in a whole new direction... just like that Rocket Man."

Nearly running across campus, Jill could hardly contain herself. She knew that whatever classes she had, she was going to have to perform well. None of this concerned her. What had her more uneasy was this audition. She couldn't wait to get back to her dorm to start researching what the rest of the requirements were, how she goes about finding a recording studio and who she can find to accompany her. She was so completely lost in thought, Jill didn't even know where she was going, and had walked past her dorm into an area she didn't recognize.

Not good, she thought. *Typical. I need to focus*. Her tendency to be hard on herself rather than forgive herself was part of the reason she was successful, but also part of the reason she often held herself back. Should she ask for directions or find her own way back? She hated looking silly. *Wait. There was that guy again.*

What are the odds of running into him again? I have another chance…

"Hey Michael," she called. He didn't hear her. "Hey Michael," she yelled louder. Mike turned around to see her waving. He acknowledged her with a wave. Jill picked up her pace and caught up to him. "I learned what I needed. Seems I can't transfer without auditioning."

"Oh, I could have told you that." Mike smiled. "I went through the exact same thing last year."

"So, maybe you can give me some pointers on what I need to do?" Jill was hopeful. If nothing else, her dad had taught her to always use everything you've got at your disposal… of course he was referring to medicine. When he served in the military as a physician, it became painfully clear that he had to be resourceful. "I'd really appreciate any help you can offer."

"Sure, no problem," said Mike. "I'm not a voice student, but I'll help where I can." Mike seemed to Jill to be shy, but if he was going to make it in the music business, he needed to develop a personal presence. Jill could help him with that. Doesn't mean he would be comfortable doing it. She was used to people like him.

After they exchanged phone numbers, Jill made her initial request. "First thing I need to know is how the hell I got all the way over here, and how do I get back to my residence hall?"

Mike showed her the way. It was the beginning of a lot of things Mike Munoz was going to show her.

* * * * *

Jill sat at the desk in her dorm room poring over her biology text book. A once-through should get her through the midterm, she thought. It had always been enough before. She never had trouble grasping written material before. She could close her eyes and visualize a shopping list her mother made for the grocery store a year ago, and remember everything that was on it, and everything her mom forgot to buy that day, including the Butterfinger bar that she had surreptitiously added to the list right before she left the house.

Kicking herself for scheduling her Biology class at nine in the morning on Mondays, Wednesdays and Fridays, Jill bemoaned the fact that she could never stay late after her music seminar and hang out with anyone at Jacobs. She had to consistently beg off invitations to go out for coffee, a drink, or to hear somebody playing or singing at a local club. She really needed to perform well that first semester on those required courses to insure her application to the music program. She was exhausted and the information wasn't staying with her. Her mind was wandering back to the plaza in front of Jacobs where she had to say goodbye to everyone just an hour before.

"Oh come on, Jill, we need you." Meagan pleaded with her. "We need your voice for this." The girls who had fast become her friends were trying to engage Jill to join them in a choral group. They were actually in the first stages of putting together a pop group, but couldn't call it that as freshmen and sophomores, as it was frowned upon for underclassmen. They wanted Jill in it so badly that they were overlooking her best interests. Meagan had come to IU from California. Her stringy blond hair as well as the rest of her appearance used to be unkempt, but after a year around school, her self-image became just as important to her as her talent. She now carried herself with confidence and pride. Jill believed that success would do that for a lot of people. Meagan befriended Jill on the first Tuesday night of the Music Theory class, having heard Jill singing to herself in the restroom.

"I have to do well on my Biology midterm." Jill defended herself. If I don't have a good GPA to go with my audition, I won't be able to get in next semester." Jill paused and looked up at the sky. She wasn't a religious person, despite the church upbringing, but she had been praying constantly that this G-d guy was going to help her with this. "If I don't get in, I'll just die."

Jill shook her head violently to try to bring her focus back to her biology book. She flipped the page back to the beginning of the chapter and started to read when her cell phone vibrated in her back pocket and then began to ring. The familiar ring tone, "You've Gotta Have Heart…" got louder and louder. She always giggled to herself when her Dad called. She had picked that ring tone for him for a few reasons: because it was a song from "Damn Yankees," one of her favorite old Broadway Shows; it was positive thinking kind of song; and last, silly enough, her dad was a 'heart man.'

"Hi Dad!" It was kind of late for him to be calling, so she was a little concerned. "Is everything okay?"

"Hi Jelly Bean." Arnie had been calling her Jelly Bean since she was a little girl. It started because she was so tiny, like a little bean, that's what he called her – "Bean." It later morphed into Jelly Bean because when she learned to talk and people asked her what her name was, she would speak so fast and so soft that 'Jill Kelly' often sounded like 'Jelly'. "Everything is fine. I had planned to call earlier, but had an unpredictable twist in a late surgery. Just got home and grabbed a sandwich, and here I am. Why, did I call too late?"

"Nope." Jill wanted so badly to tell him that she just got back from her favorite class, but he doesn't even know she's taking a music class. "Studying for my biology midterm."

"Studying! You?" Arnie was actually surprised. He knew that Jill would encounter more difficulty in college than she had in high school, but certainly not with these basic classes. He was convinced she had an eidetic memory. All she had to do was look at the page once and it became part of her intellectual memory. He figured her first challenges wouldn't arise until junior or senior year.

"You okay?"

"Yeah, Dad." She had to think fast. "I just mismanaged my time a little. Have to read a chapter or two that I hadn't gotten to yet. I'm fine."

"You had me a little concerned." The conversation turned to the same things it always did. They talked about the Panthers, mom's Book Club, Ivan and Eric, the weather, and who he could call to help her with anything. Jill cradled her phone between her ear and her shoulder, adding in an occasional 'uh huh' or 'yeah.' Arnie did love the sound of his own voice. Just as Jill began her eye roll, even though it had less impact when nobody could see it, Arnie wrapped it up with, "I'll let you get back to your reading."

"Thanks, Dad. Give mom a kiss for me." Relieved that she had survived the call, Jill allowed the phone to slip out of her neck hold, caught it with her hand and forcefully pushed the end-call button. *Gotta love him,* she thought. Leaning back against her desk chair, she began drumming her fingers on her text book. The rhythm reminded her almost of a heartbeat. BUM bum BUM bum BUM bum. Not good for hip-hop… better for a four-four standard. Or a love song.

"SHIT!" she screamed. "BACTERIA SUCKS." She slammed the book shut, jumped up from her desk and stormed out of the corner dorm room, down the hall. Nobody was around. She went into the girl's room and into a toilet stall, slamming the door behind her. When she was finished, she flushed, and went to wash her hands, one of the girls from down the hall stumbled in, carrying a big plastic cup.

"Wanna beer?" Just as she said it, everything the girl had been drinking and eating came up and spewed forcefully from her, shooting out directly at Jill. Now covered in vomit, Jill recoiled, backed away directly into one of the showers.

I had three directions I could have gone, she thought. *Study, stay at Jacobs or this.* She turned on the shower and got directly under it, fully clothed, without waiting for it to heat up, frantically trying to rinse off the vomit, the smell and the vivid memory of it hurling towards her. After ten minutes, she poked her head out. The humanitarian who shared her beer was out cold on the bathroom floor.

Jill turned off the water and grabbed a loose towel that had been hanging for days on a hook under the smoked windows. She had no idea to whom it belonged. She didn't care. It never occurred to her that the very bacteria about which she was studying might be alive and well in the towel. No Matter. She dried her hair and face first, and then made a fruitless attempt at wringing the water out of her clothes, at least enough to get her back to her room without flooding the hallway. She carefully folded up the towel and slid it under the drunken girl's head.

When she got back to her room, her roommate was there. Paula was a little bit of an isolationist. Or a snob. Jill hadn't quite figured out which one. Paula couldn't ignore this one though, and asked her what happened. As she changed into her nightshirt, Jill told a condensed version of the story, and slipped back into her desk chair. Just as she flipped open her book, Paula switched out the light.

"Really?" Jill had been through this before. "I have a midterm at nine tomorrow."

"Use your desk lamp. That's what it's for."

Paula turned her back to Jill and pulled the covers over her head.

"So, what else is new?" Jill mumbled under her breath. *What the hell is this girl's problem? I never met anybody so blatantly cold and mean. What did I do to her to deserve this shit? No wonder she doesn't have any friends.*

Jill fumbled around on her desk to find her desk lamp and switched it on low. She pulled the neck down low over her book and opened it, once again, to the same chapter with which she had been struggling earlier. Again, she found herself drumming her fingers on the desk. BUM bum BUM bum BUM bum.

Chapter 3

"Try it again." Mike had an interminable amount of patience. Jill knew he didn't think it was a good idea for her to submit the audition tape with just a tenor sax accompaniment. The piece lent itself to full orchestra or at least string quartet. But this was her audition, not his. And it was definitely unique.

"Wait. I have to clear my throat." Jill had been fighting a cold for a week, but she had to get this project done before Thanksgiving. She had no fighting chance of getting accepted into the program if she didn't get this perfect and in on time, and certainly no chance if she didn't nail her finals. Besides, her father would never grasp anything less than a 4.0 grade point average. After finals would mean no time for anything else but studying. She had let everything go up until now and was finding that college level classes were a challenge. For the first time in her life, she had received less than perfect scores on tests, essays and projects.

She put the water glass down and softly coughed into her sleeve. "Okay, let's do it."

"Star vi - no ci - bel _al - dol,- che li s' a - - ma," Clear as a bell. Mike chimed in with a very subtle and soft jazz riff underneath. "È_il più va go - dì - let - to d'a mo," she continued. Mike stopped as she reached a crescendo.

"Why'd you stop?" Jill was confused. She thought it was going well for the first time.

"You're really very good." Mike sat down. "I really didn't have the vision to see how an operatic solo would work with a tenor sax accompaniment, much less an arrangement that imposed a jazz feeling to it. It's really forward thinking and REALLY good." He paused as a look of concern washed over his face.

"Yeah, so, then what's the problem?" Jill took another sip of water.

"I just hope that the admissions committee can see the creativity, and don't turn you down because it isn't piano, and more traditional."

Jill hadn't thought of that. If using Mike's sax will eliminate her, maybe she's making a big mistake. Suddenly, she was questioning herself and was no longer confident in this decision. But where was she going to find accompaniment now? Okay, she thought. Be resourceful. Use what you've got. That's what her dad always used to tell her. *Use whatever you've got.*

"Mike, who else do you know auditioning?"

"Nobody, this semester." Mike put his hand to his chin. He always did that when he was lost in thought. Jill seemed to think it was cute that he resembled Rodin's 'The Thinker' when he was actually thinking. "Naomi can do this piece. I know she played it for at least four auditions last year."

"Who is Naomi?"

"She's a girl."

"I figured that much." Jill also knew Mike was hiding something from her when he gave her supremely vague answers. 'She's a girl' was about as vague as he could be. "An ex?"

"Yeah, and one that ended ugly. But I'm pretty sure she'd do this for you." Mike's knee started bouncing slightly, but grew faster as he spoke. "I guess I can call her for you." He started to reach around to his backpack to get his phone when Jill jumped up and lunged over to stop him. She laid right her arm over his, and she placed her left hand on his bouncing knee.

"Do it later, when I'm not around, okay?" She looked straight into his eyes, reassuring him that it was okay. She had a past, too. It wasn't like they were dating or anything. "Come on. Let's go grab a sub."

Mike relaxed both his knees and his arm. He looked relieved. Jill asked why he had seemed so shook up. He first told her how he couldn't believe how he was lucky enough to meet her, and then carefully explained his most recent past, including a painful synopsis of his relationship with Naomi. Only two years ago, in high school, he was flailing and totally lost. He had no focus, lost in an addiction, afraid of his own shadow, and mixed up with a girl who was only out for her own best interests. Dating Mike because he was going to be a doctor, Naomi was planning on studying music and they both ended up at I.U. Naomi, Jill decided, had been the supreme gold-digger, having thought Mike would be able to support her with a big fat paycheck while she tried to make it as a musician. He had only smoked an occasional blunt, but she had turned him on to cocaine and he quickly became a slave to his addiction. He only got clean over the summer before starting school, and realized then that he, too, wanted to pursue his music. That was the genesis of their parting of ways. Jill was smart enough to let him call Naomi later, so as not to put any undue pressure on him.

The two of them packed up and left the studio as they found it, all equipment stowed, all power off and all lights out. Mike had made that mistake before, having left some microphones live and a couple of lights on, and therefore lost studio privileges for a month.

They bundled up in jackets and scarves and headed out. Indiana gets a lot colder in early November than Jill was accustomed.

They strolled across campus toward the student union. Being a freshman on the dining plan, Jill only had certain places she could get food. Mike was on a limited budget so anytime he could get a free meal, he was in, so he was willing to eat anywhere.

The leaves had already reached their peak of color and had begun to fall, and with a slight wind kicking up, Jill felt the chill go through her. She was only praying she could get the audition tape done before whatever cold or flu in which she was fighting settled. Mike put his arm around her and pulled her in closer to his body. They made an awkward couple due to his height and lankiness. Her lack of stature would leave her head nestled right next to his heart. Bum BUM Bum BUM Bum BUM. She could hear his heart beat right through his jacket.

"No onions," she instructed the sandwich chef. If she bought two halves and two drinks, they could both eat on her meal ticket. "What do you want on yours?"

"Whatever… surprise me." Mike was easy to please. In fact, Mike was relaxed and laid back about almost everything, except, perhaps, his music. Music was his supreme focus. He had been studying music since he was a kid, and came from a musical family. His father, while a prominent attorney, was also an accomplished musician. His brother and sister both were musicians. The main difference between Jill and Mike is that his parents supported his desire to change his major and study music.

Jill came bouncing back to the table where Mike had settled and slid the tray across the sticky surface. "Whadduya wanna drink?" Mike shrugged his shoulders as he pulled the tray toward him.

Jill turned on her heels and sauntered in the direction of the fountain drinks, fully expecting Mike to call out something. Nothing. Just as she stopped to turn around she heard him. "Water is fine." She pivoted and grabbed two empty cups and headed back to the water fountain. Mike sat watching every move she made.

He was falling for her. Jill could tell. She didn't want to let it get in the way of their work, but she knew he thought she was special.

They sat together in silence, eating the sandwiches and drinking the water as if they were dining at a sidewalk café in Paris. The world around them didn't seem to exist. The only sound they each heard was the occasional murmur of satisfaction that one only gets from the feel of a favorite food hitting the bottom of an empty stomach. Mike finished first and crumpled the wrapper into a small ball, took aim and promptly tossed his garbage at Jill's uncovered water cup.

"Thanks," she scoffed. "I wasn't finished with that." She knew, though, that Mike could have as easily dipped her pigtails in an inkwell or punched her in the playground. This, she decided, was the only way he knew how to tell her that he was interested in more than a friendship.

"Sorry." Mike didn't know why he did it. He used to do things like that to his sister, just to aggravate her, knowing full well that it was juvenile to do so. They both chatted about the kids back in elementary school who would always be doing stuff like that to the girls; like pulling the sleeves of their coats inside out and then hanging them back in the closet, and then offering to help them with their coats; or breaking the points of their pencils off just so he could offer to sharpen them. But what had he accomplished by throwing the trash at her? "Let me go get you a fresh cup."

"That's okay. Can we go now? I have some studying to do, and if you wouldn't mind calling that Naomi girl?" Jill stood up, picking up the tray and what was left of the garbage. "I still want you to do the tape with me with just your sax, but if she can't do the piano for me as well, I need to find someone else, and I mean quick."

Mike was the one that put this idea in her head. What if they decide that she shouldn't have submitted two versions? What if his advice is the reason she doesn't get accepted? He was beating himself up over this when Jill got back from the garbage can.

"C'mon."

"Jill." Mike hesitated. "Do you think you ought to find out from the admissions office what their policy is on this before we go any further?" He looked down at his feet, and began to swallow his words. "I mean, I don't want to give you bad advice."

"Hmmmm. Not a bad idea, at all." Jill was thinking maybe this guy just didn't want to call his old girlfriend. Or maybe he didn't want to play sax for the audition tape. There it was again. The committee in her head was debating without all of the facts. "I'll call when I get back to my dorm room, and then I'll let you know."

They grabbed their bags, coats and the sax and headed for the door. When they reached the double doors of the student union, he put down his sax and backpack. He giggled to himself at the fact that the sleeves were inside out. She had been in such a hurry to get out of the jacket that she had just yanked her arms through and left it that way. Seems he didn't have to throw his garbage in her water cup after all. "May I help you with your coat?"

"Why certainly!" She wriggled into her coat, and grabbed her bag. Mike was slightly more methodical in the process. While Jill was ready to rock 'n roll, Mike was still slowly buttoning up his coat, stacking up his papers, carefully placing them in his backpack, and one at a time, lifting the straps of his instrument bag and the rest of his belongings. Jill was restless and began fumbling around in her coat pocket, pulling out a wrinkly pack of Newport cigarettes, turning her back to Mike to see if there were any left in the box.

"You really need to stop that shit." Mike wasn't unaware of her habit. "You're going to ruin that voice of yours. If not that, at least your lung capacity is going to suffer."

"I know. I know. Never mind that. You should hear my father go at me about it." Her father is so dead set against smoking, as a cardiologist he has seen so much. "If he knew I was still smoking he would kill me." She remembered back to when he caught her smoking in the back yard with some of her theater friends. He blew a gasket; banned her friends from the house; punished her with grounding her, which made her miss some of her voice classes; doubled up on her chores, including cleaning out the air-conditioning vents. He was anal about it. And she knew he was right. She snubbed out the cigarette to appease Mike, fully knowing that she wasn't going to be able to quit that easily, but it would have to do for the time being.

They had to force open the door of the student union as the wind had kicked up, heralding an early cold front. The blast of air caught Jill by surprise, and she grabbed her scarf, keeping it from blowing off her shoulder. Stuffing it in around her neck, she fell behind Mike who hadn't noticed and was walking on briskly. "Wait for me." She broke into a trot to catch up. "Are you mad at me?"

"No," Mike offered. He kept walking. "I just didn't notice that you had stopped." His mind had wandered back to his grandfather, who had to have a lung removed due to cancer, and how he wasn't there because of his addiction last year. "I just think you should stop smoking is all."

"I will." They walked back to Jill's dorm in silence.

Chapter 4

"It's your turn, Jelly Bean."   Arnie always loved this part of Thanksgiving when everyone around his table would take a few minutes to reflect on that for which they are grateful. He always spent all of Thanksgiving Day ruminating about what he would say, but only during the commercials of the myriad football games and parades. Bean always used to get up early to help Doris in the kitchen and then snuggle up with him to watch the Macy's parade. In the afternoon, the boys would join him in the "Man Cave" to watch the games while the girls put the finishing touches on Thanksgiving Dinner.

"Um," started Jill. She had rehearsed her speech this year because she had to be sure that she didn't make any mistakes, allowing anyone in on her deception.

"As always, I'm grateful for my wonderful, supportive and loving family, and mostly that I'm away from the incessant teasing of my fantastic brothers."

She was expecting a big laugh, but only DeeGee, her grandfather, reacted. Her grandfather wanted to be called something other than grandfather or grandpa, because it made him feel old, so he came up with D. G., short for Dr. Grampa. DeeGee laughed or at least reacted to anything and everything

Jill said or did. She was his only granddaughter, and he was a sap for little girls. Jill had him wrapped around her little finger, but the one thing she couldn't tell him was that she didn't want to be a doctor.

"I'm also thankful to be able to share yet another Thanksgiving weekend with DeeGee and Grandma, grateful for their good health and that they are even around to be here today."

Arnie leaned forward and squeezed Jill's hand.

"Thank you, Bean. Okay, Doris, the ball is in your court… bring it on home."

Doris stood up. Since Arnie rarely let her have a say in anything, this was her big opportunity to talk, and she intended to take full advantage. "Okay, thank you Arnie. First let me say thank God the turkey isn't dry."

Now they laughed, but it was a nervous laugh, because everyone around the table knew how sensitive Doris was about her cooking. She took it very seriously.

"This beautiful, bright family is my life's work," she began. Doris spoke for almost ten minutes talking about each member of her family and the best attributes of each. She then turned her attention to her husband, and how grateful she was for the life he had provided for all of them. She closed asking everyone to take hands and say the Lord's Prayer. By then, everything was cold, but she declared that it was time to eat! "Dig in."

Doris reached over and pulled the foil off of the turkey and lifted the lids off of all of the serving dishes. Silverware started clicking and clacking. For fifteen minutes, nobody spoke except to ask for something to be passed to them. Ivan broke the silence. "Bean, switch seats with me. I wanna watch the second half of the game."

Ivan had the remote control for the big screen TV in his back pocket and switched it on, but his back was facing the living room. "Get up and switch with me."

Doris couldn't stand his lack of manners, but before she could say anything, Arnie corrected his oldest son. "Where are your manners? How about a please? In fact, I think you can wait until after dinner. Please turn that off."

"I'm done." Ivan was sliding his chair out, with the intent of leaving the table and moving onto the living room couch.

"Ivan! Sit!" Arnie was pissed off. "You know better than that. You wait until the meal is over."

"Shit." Ivan slumped back into his chair. "Then eat, people."

There was no more discussion. In fact, Ivan had introduced the one and only rift that plagued the Kelly family. Ivan was the rebellious one; the selfish one; and the one who never wanted to follow the rules.

He sat in his chair pouting as if he were a child, yet his athletic physique and sheer girth defied his behavior.

Crossing his arms, he leaned to his right and elbowed Eric, who was casually and slowly enjoying his second helping of turkey, mashed potatoes and gravy. Grandma was reaching for another helping of green bean casserole and Jill was still working on her first plateful.

Doris jumped up and headed into the kitchen to get dessert ready to serve. "I think we can have dessert casually tonight, Arnie. If anyone wants to have a piece of pie while watching the game, I'll serve it up on a plastic plate, okay?

"No, Doris." It was if Arnie was punishing Ivan. His disappointment in Ivan's academic path shows up all the time, and was partly the reason Jill had to keep hers a secret. "This is a special holiday. When dessert is over, he can go watch the game."

Ivan's mood darkened, but he waited.

"So, Bean, how are your classes coming along?" Arnie changed the subject. "You have your finals in a couple of weeks, right?

"Everything is okay. I'm just taking the basic freshman core classes, and one elective, Dad, so it isn't really much of a challenge." Jill took a matter-of-fact attitude because anything else would have been out of character.

"The only challenge has been finding a quiet place to read. The dorm is so noisy, and it's a long cold walk to the library now that the weather has changed." *That sounded innocuous enough.* "I'm planning on getting a lot of reading done over this weekend."

"And you, Eric?" Arnie was, again, doing rounds, as if he were in a teaching hospital again. "What's doing with you? You gonna graduate on time and what about med school applications?"

"Everything's right on schedule, Dad." Eric knew the drill. It was the same every damn time he came home. "I'm figuring on a 4.0 again, and as soon as the grades are posted, I'll send out the applications. They're all ready to go."

"Where are you applying?" Arnie knew where he wanted Eric to attend medical school. There's a Kelly family tradition at University of North Carolina at Chapel Hill.

Eric hesitated, because he knew where this was going. "I've done applications to UNC, New York University, Johns Hopkins, Duke and Harvard."

"Oooooh, Harvard and Johns Hopkins! High aspirations, have we?" Arnie thought Harvard trained doctors were snobs. Eric and Jill both believed it was because he wasn't accepted into the program. Arnie never admitted that but it was true. He perpetuated this by stressing the importance of this legacy thing at UNC. His ego would never allow any other way of dealing with it.

"Dad, I'm just applying. I don't know that I'll be accepted. I'm trying to be open minded. Can you?"

Arnie's brow descended into a deep furrow. "You know what Doris, go ahead and serve the pie from the kitchen. Let everybody do whatever the hell they want. You're all excused." He forced his chair away from the table and quietly stomped, if that's possible, away from the dining room toward the back of the house.

DeeGee recognized this. He's seen it before, and he knew to let it go. "Come on kids, my mouth is watering for your mother's pecan pie. Help me clear off the table."

Chapter 5

"I got in!" Jill could hardly contain herself. She hadn't even closed her ski jacket as she stumbled across campus toward the student union. Her fingers were cold and stiff and she could barely hold onto the phone, but she just couldn't wait to call Mike. Carrying the letter from the Jacobs School in one hand, her phone in the other, she had slung her purse and backpack over the same shoulder and tripped down the steps of her dorm out into the cold December air. "I thought I had to wait until January to hear."

"No, you got your audition tape in for the January semester. They had to let you know before classes began." Mike was actually ecstatic for her, but never showed more than a matter of fact attitude about much. "Now you have to go over and do drop/add for some of your classes." He shifted from one elbow to the other so he could pull the blanket up over him and settle back into the pillow, knowing this was going to be longer a conversation than he had originally anticipated. *It was Sunday morning, for God's sakes, woman.*

"Can you help me with that?" Jill spoke in her little girl voice, knowing he would melt. Over the past three months, she had figured out that he was a sucker for her helpless act. She, too, switched hands with the phone, tugging her jacket in closer as she slowed her pace.

The wind had died down for a minute, but she was feeling the Indiana winter setting in. The trees all over campus were already bare, and the few leaves that the engineering department hadn't gotten up with those huge machines were swirling around gently. Suddenly Jill came to a stop. *What am I going to tell my parents? How do I explain the change in my classes for January? Wait, I don't have to tell them anything. They don't have to know. I have to do the undergrad requirements anyway, so if they ask, I don't even have to lie.*

Jill didn't realize how long she had been standing there, and hadn't even noticed that a light flurry of snow had started to mix in with the leaves as the wind picked up. "Hey, Jill… you still there?" Mike sat up in bed after the long silence. "You okay?"

"I'm here." Jill was suddenly in the present.

"Can I come over?" Not sure why she asked that, Jill was hoping to share her excitement with somebody. Mike was the closest friend that she had made since she had arrived at Indiana. She was finding herself more attracted to his gentleness and kindness. *Maybe I want more than just friendship.*

Maybe it isn't even about this letter. She waited for a response.

"I guess." Mike began. "I'm just now getting up, so not terribly presentable. I haven't even showered yet." Mike threw the covers off, wincing as his feet hit the cold linoleum floor. "What time will you be here?"

"I'm about ten minutes away, but if you want, I can stop at the café at the union and pick up some coffee and something for breakfast." Jill slapped her hand against the back of her backpack to be sure she had put her wallet in the outside pocket before she had left her dorm room.

"Just coffee for me." Mike was never big on breakfast, probably a result of his using days, when he would be up for two or three days at a time, without eating much of anything, and then sleeping it off for a day and a half. When he usually woke up from a run, food was never too appealing. "Not too hungry."

"See you soon!" Jill was hoping Mike could hear her smile through the phone. She always felt that it was possible to hear emotions in peoples' voices. That, she thought, was why she had always worked so hard on her phrasing and inflection when she sang. That was what was going to set her apart as a pop singer.

The door to the Union was locked on the south side, as it usually was on Sunday mornings, at least until 10:00 am. She dropped her backpack at her feet long enough to close up her jacket and tighten up her scarf knowing that when she turned the corner to the west side of the building the winds would pick up. She was already chilled to the bone and had, indeed, noticed the snowfall, as it had picked up ever so slightly.

"Two large coffees and one cheese Danish, please." Jill had walked around to the north of the building where the door was propped open by somebody's biology textbook. *Hmmm. Soon, that'll be my textbook, serving another purpose other than educating me on the wonders of bacteria.* "Can you double bag that please? It's starting to snow, and I have to get to the other side of campus and keep it hot."

Once again, the student run café had employed someone who would rather be in bed, sleeping than see to anyone else's special request. Jill thought she heard the guy grunt, indicating to her that he had not only heard but would accommodate her request. She stood on her toes, painful as that was because she was sure they were frozen solid. Nobody had told her to have thick socks. The guy was wrapping the coffee in plastic wrap so it wouldn't spill, and then several layers of paper. *Kind of like the layering that I do to keep warm... works for me.* "Thanks so much."

At least my ass is good for something. Jill pushed backwards against the door, with her backpack over her shoulder and the package from the café in her hands. *At least I remembered to button up this time.* The rest of the walk wasn't too bad. Jill was shielded from the wind by the library building, and Mike lived just on the other side of the quad up near Tenth Street. She was hoping Mike was ready for her because waiting around the lobby of that place gave her the creeps. Some of those guys act like they've never seen a female before.

Jill balanced the coffee on the doorknob of Mike's apartment, and gently knocked on the door. At least she didn't have to deal with a roommate. It was hard enough for her to cope with her own roommate. "You there?"

"Yup!" Mike had answered the door, wrapped in one towel with another wrapped around his head. Startling Jill, he had to dive to catch the package from the café as it teetered and slid from its precarious position on the doorknob. They both grabbed at the same time, flipping the bag over a complete 360 turn as it landed on the floor. "Shoot." Mike bent over to pick up the bag. "I'm sorry; I didn't mean to scare you."

"That's okay. I just hope it didn't spill all over my Danish." She laughed to herself, thinking that this was the guy to whom she was attracted. The turban wrap around his long hair was starting to slide to one side. He looked so cute to her, but she didn't want to embarrass him so she quickened her pace, kicked the door open and snatched the bag from him so he could keep his towel from falling off completely. "You want a few minutes to get dressed?" Jill always saw him as shy, but at this particular moment, that was gone.

"Okay with me if it's okay with you if you want to come in." Mike had become less blasé about their friendship. Nobody else was stirring on the floor of his apartment building and he didn't seem to be intimidated by the circumstances. He hated having to use a community bathroom, because it wasn't a lot different than living in the dorms, but at least he didn't have to live by anyone else's rules. While it was a tiny studio, it was his.

"See if you can find a place to sit down." Never having seen the inside of a man's bedroom other than her brothers' when she was growing up, Jill was expecting something slightly different. Having grown up with two brothers, she anticipated either a mess like Ivan used to have, or the absolute meticulousness she saw in her brother Eric. Mike, it turned out, was somewhere in between.

He didn't have any posters of sports heroes, or even musicians for that matter, hanging on his walls. He had saxophones. Four of them. And a few other musical instruments.

Mike's desk was piled high, albeit neatly, with music scores, notebooks and textbooks. The trashcan was empty, but there were a few dirty glasses a plate left on a small table in the corner. What she noticed was lacking were clothes and shoes. There was nothing thrown over a chair or shoved under the bed. Everything, from what she could see in a cursory glance around the room, was either folded on a shelf or hung neatly in the closet. The bed was left unmade, but she could forgive Mike that because, after all, she did wake him early on a Sunday morning.

I should have just called him last night when I checked the mail.

Jill sat down on the chair by the table in the corner with her back to Mike as he slipped on some boxers and a pair of jeans. She tried to look as though she was occupying herself with something in front of her so she wouldn't have a reason to turn around. It dawned on her that she could slip her phone out of her backpack which was leaning up against her chair. She reached down to get it, trying to unzip it without looking down, but she couldn't find the right pocket.

"Need help with that?" Mike had stepped up behind her, having thought better about getting completely dressed, in only his boxers. He picked up the back pack and handed it to Jill, without allowing her to see that he was not dressed. When she turned to take it from him, her eyes were met head on with his plaid flannel boxers, bulging ever so slightly in the middle. She slowly tilted her head back, her eyes tracing a path up Mike's slender torso which was still glistening with the dampness remaining from his morning ablutions.

"Umm…"

Mike leaned over, allowing the backpack to slide gently from his grip, and carefully placed his face precariously close to hers. Her first thought was to kiss him, having been looking forward to this moment for a long time. She stopped herself. She didn't want to be the aggressor. She didn't want him to think this was something she did often. In fact, this would be her first time. She wasn't sure if she was feeling exhilaration, panic or sexual tension. All she knew was that her heart was beating wildly; she had butterflies in her stomach and growing warmth and twitching between her legs.

He did it. He finally did it. He arched his neck in and kissed her, tentatively. She didn't pull back. She didn't push back. She just let him. She parted her lips enough to let him know it was okay and he gently slipped his tongue in, exploring carefully and sensually the inner reaches of her mouth. Mike pulled away and without a sound reached out his hand to Jill. Leading her to his unmade bed, he turned her around, silently slipping off her coat and unwrapping her scarf. He took her in her arms and pulled her close holding her stiffly, but carefully, like a tray of filled glasses.

"You okay with this?" Mike looked deeply into Jill's eyes. He had always been told he was good at reading people, and before he went any further, he was trying to study her. Jill let him know not only with her eyes, but by pulling him closer and grinding against him, looking for his lips with hers. She wasn't really sure what to do, but this action seemed natural.

They stood there together, lost in each other until Jill kicked off her shoes, reached down and unzipped her own jeans, and wriggled out of them until they were a heap on the floor. Mike helped her with her shirt lifting it over her head, his turban towel dropping to the floor. He pulled her down on top of him on the bed, and gently pulled the covers over them.

* * * * *

My arm is completely numb. I can't move my fingers. Jill thought to herself, half asleep.

She wasn't awake enough to realize where she was, too foggy to remember what had happened. *Must have slept on it funny.* But when she tried to move it, she couldn't, so she opened her eyes to see Mike lying on top of her arm, facing her, asleep. He was breathing deep and steady and he had a hint of a smile across his face. His long, brown locks, still slightly damp from his shower, were spread across the pillow behind him.

Jill tried to slide her arm out from under him without waking him. Having a modicum of success, with Mike only sighing and snuggling into the pillow, she slid out of the side of the bed and quickly tried to get dressed. Glancing around the room, she looked for bra but it was nowhere in sight. *Must be under the covers. Oh well, I can do without.* She was taken aback by how cold Mike's apartment was. She walked soundlessly to the window and saw something she had not seen in a long time. The ground was covered with a dusting of snow, yet just enough had settled on the car hoods to make snowballs.

"Mike, get up."

She drove across the room and pounced on the empty side of the bed. She couldn't rouse him as Mike was in a deep sleep. She discovered her bra sticking out from under the pillow, gently tugged at it to free it from its bondage.

Funny, it's free now, only to hold me hostage, she thought as she pulled her arms back through her sleeves, slipped her arms through the straps of the bra, wriggled her arms around the back to hook it together, and then slipped her arms back through the sleeves.

Jill was just about finished dressing when Mike rolled over, half awake. She could tell there would be no convincing him to get up, get dressed and come with her to have a snowball fight. "I need to get back to my dorm room. I have some more studying and reading to do before tomorrow. Remember," she added,

"I still have two finals to take."

Swallowing his words and stretching, Mike responded with a grunt. "Mmmm okay, bye." Rolling back over, he covered his head with a pillow and let out a contented sigh.

That's all there is? I come over here to celebrate the biggest turning point in my life, give myself to you, and all you can do is roll over and go back to sleep?

Jill was feeling somewhat remorseful. She hadn't ever done something like this before. She had never gone this far with a guy before, had sex before. Her judgment was clouded.

But I got into Jacobs! So, what if he went back to sleep? So, what if I lost my virginity? I'm on my way...

Jill tripped down the stairs and out the front door of Mike's apartment into the mid afternoon sun, glistening off the top of parked cars. The snow had stopped, and hadn't accumulated much, but it was still cold enough to stick to the metal hoods. She stopped at the first car, threw her backpack and purse over her shoulder, and gathered just enough off of the hood to make a small snowball. She spun around a hurled it at the stop sign at the end of the parking lane. That seemed to be just enough to satisfy her curiosity.

Chapter 6

"Dammit. I have to change that ringtone." Jill jumped up out of bed and grabbed her phone to try to turn off the ringer, but it was too late. Paula, the shrew, was already bitching at her.

"Can't you change that, or at least turn it down?" Paula rolled over with only one eye open. She had grown to despise her roommate, likely out of jealousy, Jill believed. Paula was probably barely passing her classes, had no idea what major to pursue, had few friends and certainly didn't have a boyfriend.

Jill, on the other hand, knew exactly what she wanted to do with her life. She had surrounded herself with like-minded people who had similar goals, and when she wasn't studying, she was over at the Music School hanging out with them, singing, writing songs and making lifelong friends and important business connections that would eventually propel her forward in her career. Further, she was in love. Not only was she in love, but she was getting laid! Paula could use a good tumble in bed, Jill believed. It might just loosen her up a little.

"Really, Paula, its noon on a Saturday. It's not so unreasonable that my phone rang," Jill started. Thinking better of it, and not wishing to get involved with her acid tongue, she added. "You know what?

You're right. I'll try to remember to turn the ringer lower in the future." Jill got up out of bed grabbed her robe and her phone and slipped out into the hallway.

"Dad?" She was trying to tie the robe shut when her father answered.

"Morning, Bean." There was a pause. Somehow, Jill knew this wasn't good. "Sorry to bother you. I know you like to sleep half the day away on Saturdays, but I thought you should be aware… DeeGee is in the hospital." Arnie cleared his throat. "He passed out last night. We thought it was his sugar, but apparently, he had a stroke."

"Is he okay?" Jill could feel her heart pounding. DeeGee was never one to complain, so if there was something going on with him, he wouldn't have let anyone know. "How bad was the stroke?"

"Pretty bad. He's not awake." Arnie tried to choke back the emotion because he rarely showed it to his kids. "He didn't show any signs at dinner. There was no slurring, no disorientation, nothing."

"So, when did he pass out?"

"We were watching an old John Wayne movie in the den, and he suddenly stood up and started to say he was tired. And then he just collapsed." Arnie took a deep breath.

"At first I thought it was his heart, you know me." *You always think it's the heart.* "So, I tried CPR while we called emergency…" His voice trailed off.

"Do you want me to come home?" Jill loved her grandfather desperately, and she would get on a plane right away, but she was hoping her dad would say no. *Tonight's my first ever professional gig. Please, Please, Please say no.*

"Not necessary, Bean, until we know more." Jill let out a sigh of relief, peppered with guilt.

"Okay, Dad, just please keep me aware of what's happening. Jill lightly touched the 'end call' button on her phone, but stared at it for what seemed an eternity. She saw only her reflection in the smudged screen. Paula forced her way out the dorm room door, pushing right through Jill as if she weren't there, and Jill didn't even notice.

Jill looked upward and simply mouthed the words, "please, God, let him be okay." She turned and went back into her room, deflated. *"I can pray all day, but I'm also going to change my set tonight, and sing his favorite song... that's if I don't have to go home."*

Slipping into her jeans and a sweater, Jill attempted to be out of there before Paula returned from the bathroom.

She had no desire to get into it with her about ANYTHING. She needed Mike, or at least a friendly face. She grabbed her garment bag, her backpack, her purse and her phone, and slipped out the door and down the back stairs. She had everything she needed so she wouldn't have to come back there until tomorrow morning at the earliest.

It was considerably cooler outside than she was expecting. May in Indiana wasn't the same as May in North Carolina. Spring wasn't completely there on a regular basis. *Maybe this was just a cool front.* Yesterday she was in a sweatshirt, but today she could have used a heavier jacket. She bounded out across campus towards Mikes apartment. He would probably be up and hungry.

"Time flies when you're having fun." Jill could hardly believe she was almost finished her freshman year as she navigated her way through what had now become a familiar path. *I don't get lost anymore, at least.* Her folks were perfectly happy with her 4.0

her first semester, and have no idea what she's been up to this semester. *Funny how they don't even ask about my classes anymore.*

Arnie and Doris had their hands full with Ivan, who was having all kinds of problems finding work to support himself. He didn't get drafted into the minor leagues, he didn't make any of the teams he tried out for as a walk on, and he failed miserably learning anything of value in the sports business classes he took.

Isn't it just like my brother to be so cocky and full of himself? I think he thinks the world owes him a living. One of those millennials who think they're entitled? Is that the word used to describe it?

Ivan is living at home, working at an Office Depot stocking shelves.

Poor Arnie. This must be destroying him. That's what he said I would end up doing if I got a degree in music. Just wait, Daddio…. Just you wait.

"Shit!" Jill had walked right past Mike's apartment building. She couldn't figure how that had happened. Doubling back she started humming. It was a new tune. Something she didn't recognize. She liked it.

"You up yet?" She knocked on Mike's door.

"Will you let me in even if I didn't stop for coffee?" No answer. "Mike, I need to talk to you."

Jill turned on her heels, deciding to check down the hall when Mike nearly bowled her over, once again wearing just a towel. Things had cooled off between them and the relationship was evolving into a professional, musical and business partnership more than anything else.

They had only slept together two or three times since Jill had returned from North Carolina in March. It seemed to suit Mike fine. Jill, however, had fallen for him. Now, she needed him… his tenderness, his sweetness, his moral support.

"Hi."

"What's the matter, superstar?" Mike saw the stress in Jill's face. It wasn't the gig, he knew that. She was more than ready. They had been rehearsing night and day for weeks. He was convinced this was her launch. "You okay? You look panicked."

"My grandfather… DeeGee… had a bad stroke last night. I'm waiting to hear how he's doing." She took a deep breath as she pushed by him into his room. "I may have to blow off the gig and fly home."

"Shit…" Mike realized as soon as he said it that Jill might misunderstand his reaction. "I mean about your grandpa… not the gig."

"I know." Jill sat down on the edge of Mike's unmade bed. That was one thing about Mike that still irritated her. He was a slob. "Could you just hold me for a few minutes?" Mike hesitated.

"Don't worry. I just need a little comfort." Jill was really hoping for more, but she didn't want to push Mike. She patted the mussed blanket next to her, motioning him to sit.

With her head nestled against his chest, she heard that familiar beat. That comforting familiar sound that made her feel so safe and comfortable way back in the fall. BUM bum BUM bum

BUM bum. She began tapping her foot to the same beat. "I can hear your heart beat… I can feel your heart feel, I can know your thoughts as if we were one…"

"What??? What's that?"

"It's going to be my first non-cover hit song. And you're going to help me write and produce it." She stood up. She grabbed his hands and pulled him up to his feet. "Mike, I know we cooled things off, but I have had this song in my head since the day I met you. It just came together… just now." She hugged him as tight as possible, pressing her head against his chest. BUM bum BUM bum BUM bum. "I love you." BUM bum BUM bum BUM bum.

"You really are nuts." Mike pulled away. "I really care about you too, but love?"

"No, not that way…." She pressed her head against his chest once more. The beat seemed to be considerably faster now. BUM bum BUM bum BUM bum.

"I mean I love your heartbeat and that it inspired this… come on, let's get something down. Grab some paper."

Jill was so overcome with enthusiasm; she couldn't wait for him. She rummaged through a pile on his desk and found a pad of music paper.

"Can I put some clothes on first?" Mike was almost laughing at her. She hadn't shown this kind of passion since they finished her first professional music video and then made love on the studio floor. He really did care about her. She was going to something special in the music industry, and she knew she wanted him to be a part of it all.

Jill's phone remained silent for the three hours they spent trying to craft her first original pop song. They kept going over and over the verses and chorus, switching keys and transitions, dumping lyrics and writing new. She kept pausing, expecting to hear that familiar ringtone, but it didn't come. They didn't have much time left before they had to leave for the gig. Jill decided to call and check in before she committed to singing.

"Dad? Any news?" Jill asked tentatively, afraid to find out anything. Her mother always used to tell her that no news is good news, and she hadn't heard anything since this morning. She paused, breathlessly.

"Well, he awoke for a short while, but then went out again, so they haven't had a chance to do any real assessment." Arnie sounded flat. He must have been exhausted, having been at the hospital with his father through the night, with no relief from his wife or son. *How selfish*, Jill thought. *But then, that's Ivan.*

"They are planning a scan in about an hour. We'll know more then. I can call you later this evening with those results. In the meantime, Bean, sit tight."

"You sure you don't want me to come home?" Jill thought that by at least offering, she would have less guilt about wanting to stay in Bloomington at least until tomorrow.

"I told you I would let you know." Arnie seemed agitated. "You do what you have to do up there."

"Okay Dad, but please keep me posted. Tell DeeGee I love him."

Jill was misty eyed when she hung up, not sure if she was feeling sad over her grandfather or if she was feeling as though she had been reprimanded by her father. It was almost as if he was telling her to stay away, that he didn't want her there.

Was he angry at me? Did I do something wrong? Of course, I did... does he suspect something?

Jill was starting to let her thoughts run away with her again. "Hey. Hey. Are you still here?" Mike was sitting on the desk chair, on top of two or three dirty shirts that never made it to the hamper. "Sounded like things are stable there. Come on. We're not far from having something to actually make a demo."

Jill shook her head as if to jog herself back into the present. "Sorry. Was just a little concerned." "Okay… I don't think I like the transition at the end of the verse. It doesn't leave a good segue into the chorus; unless we're going to write in two verses between chorus, and then finish with a double chorus; and I think I want to slow it down, may try it in minors?"

"Huh?" Mike was completely baffled. "That makes it a totally different song."

"My song. I just want to try it, that's all." Jill was tired and irritable. "You know what? Let's put it away. I want to take a quick nap before we leave. Obviously, you think I'm making bad decisions." Jill turned around and moved toward the bed. "Can I lie down here?

"Sure." Mike was less than enthusiastic, but he did appreciate the fact that Jill recognized when she should stop working. She knew her idea was not good. Instead of admitting it, she knew she needed a nap. "Mind if we share the bed?"

Mike lay down and Jill nestled under his arm, head pressed against his chest. BUM bum BUM bum BUM bum. Within two minutes, she had fallen into a deep sleep.

The sunlight flickered across the ceiling ever so slightly, heralding the passage of enough time to refresh yet alarm Jill as she opened one eye and then the other. When she turned her head to the left on the pillow, she saw Mike in the desk chair with his back to her, his slim silhouette casting a slight shadow on the wall. He was gently tapping a pencil on the desk, lost in thought. *Or was it a melody. With Mike I never know.*

"What time is it?" She sat up abruptly, throwing the blanket off her. "We're going to be late."

"Relax, Jill. We have plenty of time." Mike hadn't even turned around. It was easier to mask his anticipation and excitement that way. The last thing he wanted to do was put any doubt or fear in Jill's head. He knew a whole lot more about this "gig" than he had told her.

His connections in the jazz world were coming tonight, and they wouldn't be alone. This was not only his shot, but Jill's as well, at getting a foot in the door in the business.

"I still need to shower and warm up my voice." Mike's calm demeanor usually worked on her, but not this time. Besides her worry about her grandfather, she wasn't sure she was ready for this. She had performed thousands of times, but never professionally. She was actually going to come home with a chunk of change in her pocket. *Well,* she thought, *not a chunk of change… but it's the first hundred bucks I've ever made singing.*

"Bahda bahda bahda. Neenee neenee neenee. Bahda bahda bahda. Neenee neenee neenee." Jill tilted her head back and let the warm water wash over her face. Her mind was drawing a blank. She couldn't remember any of the vocal exercises other than Bahda bahda bahda. Neenee neenee neenee. She did them every day but her mind was blank. *Nerves*.

"You almost done?" Mike poked his mouth through a narrow crack in the door of the women's bathroom. He knew Jill would lose herself in thought. This was always the start of her panic or anxiety attacks and he wanted to interrupt the behavior before it got started.

"Oh, yeah, Mike?" He had startled her, and wondering how long she had been in there, she reached for the knobs and immediately turned off the water. "Be right there."

Jill was ready within minutes, giving them time to stop and grab a sub on the way. That had become their signature meal. Italian cold cuts, with provolone, no onions or peppers, light oil on whole wheat. Jill tried to convince herself that this was healthy eating, having most of her meals either in the studio or at her desk. At least she wasn't scarfing down hamburgers and fries anymore.

There would be no bad breath from onions and no indigestion from fries tonight.

* * * * *

"Geez Mike, it's mobbed. Is that normal for this place?" Jill was starting to feel light headed. They were already backstage, and it smelled of beer and gasoline. *Not a safe place to light up*, she thought. "I need to drink something with a little sugar in it. Can I get a ginger ale or something?" Soda would make her hiccup. "Maybe just some water?"

Jill peeked out again. She spotted George Clooney. *How did he know I was singing tonight? Stop being so egotistical, you jerk. He probably hangs out here all the time. He didn't come just to see you. He told you he loves music and hanging out in the local clubs. Jerk.* She looked again, but she didn't see him. *Maybe it was my imagination.*

She took a deep breath and blew it out slowly. "Mike, how long until we go on?" He was cleaning his sax and fooling around with the mouthpiece. He was totally oblivious to anything going on around him. Jill repeated the question, louder, but he still didn't respond.

"Oh, hey, Buddy." Mike looked up as the owner of the club came backstage. "How have you been doing?" Buddy was a middle-aged hippie, it seemed to Jill. He was an institution in Bloomington, having studied music at Indiana, but never wanted to leave the college town or the college life. He spent the last twenty years hanging around town, playing the local clubs, his music evolving with the times, until he finally opened his own little club, booking mostly students to give them an opportunity for some stage experience. Some pretty famous musicians have played on this stage, and now Jill Kelly, a nobody from North Carolina, was going to sing there too.

"Well, hi there, Mikey." Buddy lit up a joint, inhaling deeply. His next few words snuck out of his mouth as he tried to hold the smoke in. "How's it going? Who have you got tonight?" His face was turning red, and he gave in, forcefully thrusting the balance of the smoke out into the dimly lit room. "Want a hit?"

"No thanks, Bud. Not doing that shit anymore." Mike said that easily enough, though Jill knew he wanted to get high before going on. "This is my friend Jill. Wait till you hear the pipes on her." He carefully laid his sax down on the chair beside him stood up and wrapped his arms around his old friend, whispering something into his ear.

"You got it." Buddy took another hit, and offered the dwindling joint to Jill. She put her hand up smiling, and then moved it to her throat, motioning as though she was protecting herself. "No problem. You want me to introduce you or will Mikey?"

"Think I'll let Mike do it." Jill answered quickly. She hadn't even thought about that. She knew she didn't want to use her real name, and hadn't yet decided on any kind of stage name. The last thing she wanted to do was to have someone who knows the family discover that she's performing and it get back to her parents. *There's nothing wrong with me having a little fun singing on the side, but I don't want to lose my "free tuition."*

Buddy spun around and opened the heavy side door to the club, turning back while taking one last hit. "Okay then, you guys are on in about five minutes."

Jill felt her sandwich inching up her insides into her throat. It was a relatively new feeling for her. Stage fright wasn't something she had dealt with often. Maybe it was the fact that she was doing this all surreptitiously. She swallowed hard and gently cleared her throat.

"Mike," she started. "I don't want to be introduced by my real name." There, she said it.

Mike looked at her, cocked his head to the side, and half squinting, said, "okay." Jill loved it that he accepted just about everything she said, generally with no questions. He stared at her, pensively, but this time he had to know more. "How come?"

"I guess you were going to find out sooner or later." Jill told him, in very brief terms, that nobody in her family knew she was studying music, but explaining the reasons would take too long, and they only had a couple of minutes before they went on. That seemed to keep him satisfied.

There was a soft knock at the door. It could have been a jack-hammer. Jill jumped. Mike picked up his sax and a small towel and motioned to her. "This is it kiddo… your big break."

He laughed as he led her through the big door to the side of the stage.

"Evenin' everyone!" Buddy was buzzed.

"Welcome to the Hoosier Harmony Club. We have a cool Saturday night lined up for you tonight. Some old friends and some new talent we've discovered. In honor of that, for the next hour, all drinks are half off." Buddy glanced over to our side of the stage and then to the other. "We're going to open tonight with the Mike Munoz Combo for a short set while you all get settled in. Mike…"

The audience erupted. Mike turned to Jill, smiling. "They know me here." He grabbed his stuff and started out. "Wait. What do you want me to call you? You never said. We're going to do the warm-up and then I'll introduce you and you come out."

"Just call me Jay Bee. I'll explain later."

Mike turned and joined the rest of his guys on the stage, who had already begun playing a four-four beat. When Mike walked out, the applause began again; he nodded, picked up his sax, and with his elbow, motioned to the guys to slow it down. The low, subtle, stream started and the crowd seemed mesmerized.

Boy, does he have them.

They played a six minute medley, lifted it to a crescendo and finished with a wailing solo by Mike. After a long applause with Mike nodding in each direction, he quietly turned around, picked up a towel and gently dabbed his brow. This was Mike's signature tell that he was getting ready to change pace. He peeked over toward Jill and lifted his eyebrows. She smiled, took a deep breath and bobbed her head.

Mike took the microphone out of its stand, prepared to hand it directly to Jill so there would be no chance of her fumbling with it. She had told him of the one time she tried to sing in the club and just when she was supposed to come in, the cord fell out of the mike and she had to bend over and try to put it together. She missed her cue to come in, frazzling her so much she couldn't find a place to start singing, and she had gotten so overwhelmed that she simply left the stage.

"Thanks everyone for that warm welcome. It's great to be back at the Harmony Club. It has been way too long." Mike sounded so smooth and relaxed in front of a crowd. Jill was caught by surprise because he was so shy in social situations. "I'd like to introduce a very special friend of mine, who has kindly agreed to join me tonight to regale us with her lovely voice. Please give a warm to my friend, Jay Bee."

The audience didn't seem to be as forthcoming and responsive to Jill as they had been to Mike. But then, she wasn't him. She also came to find out later that she wasn't the first 'guest' singer he has introduced. The last time he tried this, it didn't work out well. Naomi, his old girlfriend played keyboard and sang with him last year, and apparently bombed, mainly because she was so high she was unable to remember lyrics or even melodies.

This is me, not her. Jill was talking to herself as she walked out onto the stage. When they were there rehearsing yesterday, the stage seemed so much bigger. She was on top of Mike so quickly. Or was she walking faster. She reached for the Mike, smiling, and then leaned in and gave him a kiss on the cheek. The drummer kicked in with a low, steady beat. Next the bass joined in; then the trumpet and bass sax, then Mike. Jill waited a few extra measures, and then it was her turn.

She started out tentatively, but when her eyes met Mikes, and he could see them sparkling, she knew it was good. She dropped her shoulders, connected with her soul, and let loose. The people seated at the front row of tables were frozen, motionless. Nobody was making a sound except the soulful wail of Mike's sax and the soft patter of the background beat to which she had been practicing for weeks. Even the servers and bartenders had stopped their work. Her only thought was being able to hit and hold that last note.

And there it was. The reverberation of the music died out. The audience was silent for what seemed like an eternity. There was a sudden burst of cheering from the left side, and then the right and quickly, everyone was standing, clapping, whistling. "More, more."

Jill was astounded. She didn't have long to drink it in. Russ kicked in on the drums, then Sandy on the bass, and they were into the second number. The night flew by and the place was hopping. After the twenty minute set, Jill's legs were like rubber, her heart pounding, her mouth dry.

Mike leaned into the microphone and said," we'll be back in a little while." He took Jill by the hand, rested his sax against a stool and grabbed his towel. He squeezed her hand as he led her from the stage. "You did it, kiddo. You did it."

Pacing back and forth in the green room, Jill could hardly contain herself. "When do we get to go back on?" She couldn't get enough of it. The room only had two hundred people in it but she may as well have been playing at Madison Square Garden or the Hollywood Bowl.

"Easy, easy, Jay Bee." Mike had to calm her down. There were two other acts that were getting a chance to play before they went back on to close the evening. They wouldn't be back on for another hour. "Hey, that should be enough time for you to explain a little of this 'Jay Bee' stuff to me. Why aren't you using your name?"

Jill carefully laid out an explanation, trying to keep it from being too emotionally charged. She didn't want Mike to think there were serious family issues. Because there weren't, other than the fact that she was living a total lie. "I really didn't want to study to become a doctor, least of all a cardiologist," she started. "My brother Eric is the only one that knows I'm here specifically because of Jacobs, and that I'm not really pre-med. He's in the middle of applying to med school, and he DOES want to be a cardiologist, so he's promised to help me let my folks down gently, just not now."

"But when?" Mike had a conscience. He was working a 12-step program to stay clean and sober, so he wasn't really cool with all of this, especially if she was going to ask him to lie for her.

"I just need to get some kind of science degree from here, that's all. Then I tell them I'm in med school in New York, while I try to break into music. Even if I have to wait tables to get by, I'm doing this." Jill was adamant. "And no, Mike, you don't have to lie for me. You don't even have to see any of my family if you don't want to." Jill was pretty convinced that their personal relationship had become a strictly professional one at this point, so there was no point in pushing him anymore.

"What's that supposed to mean?" Mike acted as if he was on a different plane. "I'm going to want to meet the family someday, aren't I?"

Jill looked deeply into his eyes. She had been so wrapped up in making music, it never dawned on her that it could have been her that was sloughing off the relationship. *That's why his lyrics were more like love songs than soft jazz.* "Whatever. I don't want my father to stop helping with tuition, otherwise I can't stay at Jacobs. I'd never be able to afford it."

The two of them sat silently in the green room, deep in their own thoughts, both sipping hot drinks and resting. Jill was exhausted from the electricity and energy spent in just a twenty minute set. She had to recover and renew before she went out and did the second set.

* * * * *

"DeeGee is doing much better this morning." Arnie had called extremely early Sunday morning. Jill rolled over looking for her cell phone.

At least it wasn't Paula awakened by that awful ringtone. *I must change that, damn it.*

"I'm thrilled, Dad." Jill sat up in bed, trying to get her other arm out from under Mike. He was still in a deep sleep. "Sorry it took so long for me to answer. We were all out late last night and for the first time in a long time, I actually slept in this morning." Jill tried to sound matter-of-fact. Besides Eric, of all the people she really wanted to tell about last night, it was her Daddio.

"Listen, Dad. As long as DeeGee is okay, I'm thinking of not coming home after finals. A bunch of us were thinking about going over to upstate New York to do some hiking, and then down into the city for a Broadway weekend.

A friend of ours has some all-access passes for matinees, and we can see a couple of shows cheap." She waited for a response.

Arnie was quiet. He loves it when all the kids are home at once, and the beginning of summer break for all three schools just happened to coincide this year. "Are you sure? Both the boys will be in town."

"Awww, really?" She tried to sound genuine. "I don't want to let my posse down. They are my study group from biochemistry and we all need to let loose after this year."

"Okay, I guess classes are getting a little more demanding, huh?" Arnie wasn't surprised. He remembered hitting a brick wall in undergrad, but not quite this early. "You okay? I mean, are you spreading yourself too thin?"

"I'm doing great, Dad. Just need to get out and get some fresh air and entertainment. It's been a long winter. We're all ready for a break."

"All right, then. And I guess you want me to be the one to break the news to your mother."

"Yup." Jill let out a small sigh of relief. She knew she wasn't going home as far back as January.

"Thanks, Dad. Love you."

Chapter 7

How in the hell am I ever going to pull this off? Jill was frantic.

Here it was the spring of her junior year, and she was fully immersed in the Jacobs School of Music in an intensive vocal training program, taking very few outside classes, and now her parents were coming to Bloomington to visit. She hadn't even told them that she had moved off campus and was living with Mike in their dingy little one-bedroom apartment with a broken oven and no windows in the bedroom.

Mike hadn't gotten home from the corner food store, although his idea of breaking the news to Arnie and Doris about him, about her redirection of studies, about everything was not a good idea. Jill was falling apart. She was pacing instead of cleaning up. She was panicking instead of making up the bed. Her folks were staying at a little motel near campus, thinking they would be visiting her dorm. How was she going to keep them from doing that?

Paula. I'll call Paula.

Jill had moved out of the dorm in October to live with Mike, and never informed the Resident Assistant. Paula had the room to herself.

She wouldn't mind me moving back in for the weekend, would she? I'm going to call her. No, I'm not. Not this early. She's such a bitch in the morning.

Picking up the blanket off the floor, Jill started to calm down, deciding that she had found a partial solution. The next step would be convincing Mike that this wasn't the time to divulge all of her secrets. Arnie would explode.

The last time she was home, for DeeGee's funeral, he was already a little suspicious of a couple of things, grilling her about her classes and offering to 'make a few calls' if she was having trouble. Why did one of his medical school buddies have to take a teaching position at Indiana anyway? She had to have the conversation at that point. THE conversation. He had asked her where she was applying to Medical School. She had told him UNC, of course, and then she threw in a few others so that she had something to fall back on. She would have to convince him that she didn't need him to intercede, yet, but if she did, she would let him know. She remembered thinking that she would have to do some research on Medical Schools, admission requirements, MCAT scores and anything else that would make it all sound natural.

Jill tossed the blanket over the unmade bed carelessly, convinced now that her parents would never have to see the bedroom of this apartment.

I mean, I can introduce them to Mike and tell them he's my boyfriend. I can do that much.

She walked around to the other side of the full-sized bed, picked up the pillows and casually tossed them up to the headboard.

Mike walked in just as she spun around with an armful of dirty laundry to toss in the hamper. "You haven't gotten very far," he said. "I picked up some fresh chicken. I figured we could fry it on the stove top, and at least offer your folks a home cooked meal." He put the two bags carefully down on the cluttered counter. "Didn't get much done in here, either I see. By the way, do you know how to make fried chicken?"

"Funny guy." Jill was not finding his dry sense of humor the least bit funny.

"Listen, Mike. I've been thinking."

Mike got suddenly pensive. This was a usual sign that he was in some kind of trouble, or was going to be asked to do something that didn't sit well. Jill has developed a habit of 'thinking' a lot lately. He was beginning to feel the pressure of being a part of her big lie, and was truly looking forward to unfolding all of this to her family this weekend.

"I don't think I'm ready to tell my parents that I'm not studying anymore pre-med courses. I'm not prepared to handle the cost of my education and there are very few scholarships available, in fact, none for juniors at Jacobs." She sat down on a rickety chair at the card table they had been using in the "dining" room. Jill's type "A" personality compelled her to have specific rooms for activities of daily living, like eating, sleeping and cooking. Although the living room/dining room space was miniscule in their apartment, it was, because of her, clearly delineated.

"I want them to meet you, though." This was offered up as almost a consolation prize. Jill was very much aware of Mike's discomfort in living her lie. "But you can't tell them you're studying music just yet. Tell them you're undecided or something."

"Really, Jill? Really?" Mike was visibly angered. He leaned one hand on the counter and the other on his hip. "You really expect me to lie to YOUR parents about MY major?" The furrow in his brow reminded her of Leonard Bernstein. "They really think music is such a waste?" He crossed his arms on his chest, and stood firm. "Not gonna do it. If you are that afraid of your parents, then you are not the girl I thought you were. I mean, think about it. I'm a big boy. If they are going to judge me, I can stand up for myself.

If they are going to judge you for dating me, what does that say about them? Or you, for that matter?" He turned and walked heavily into the bedroom, shutting the door behind him.

"Mike, don't have a tantrum." Jill called after him. "We need to talk this through before they get here."

"I'm using the fucking bathroom, for god's sake. Calm down."

Jill continued the conversation through the closed doors. "Okay, you're right about this. But I never told them anything about you. So how can I be living with you?" Jill stepped back and fell over the couch when she got his response."

"What the hell?" He screamed loud enough that the neighbors above began stamping their feet. "They don't even know you were dating me? Geez, Jill. It's been a year and a half."

"I'm so sorry. I had them convinced I had no time for dating because of studying." She paused, but there was silence. "I'm going to see if Paula will let me stay back in my old room with her just for the weekend. I can introduce you to them, but we can't let on that it's been that long of a relationship, okay?"

More silence

The door slowly opened. Mike stepped out, drying his hands on a paper towel and then tossing it over her toward the kitchen garbage can. Cocking his head to the side, he said softly, "You really want to be a singer, don't you?"

Mike really loved Jill. He did understand the genesis of all of her motivation, and he didn't want to be the one to stand in her way. But he didn't want to sacrifice his own integrity either, with her family or professionally. He stood in the doorway, quietly in thought, watching her as she tried to regain her dignity from her position on the other side of the couch.

"Okay," he started. "Do you want me to call Paula and see if we can work something out?" He was trying to be helpful, but he was already braced for Jill's response.

"No! Absolutely not." Jill was standing now, ready to take on yet another hoax. "She already doesn't like you because I have a boyfriend and she doesn't. In fact, she hates me for it." Jill stopped, and then started again. This was common as she hatched her plans. "I'm still paying for the room so I have every right to use it whenever I want. There's no need to go to her to 'work something out.' The problem will come up only if my parents want to see the room."

Jill crossed over to Mike, giving him a quick, matter-of-fact hug on her way into their cluttered bedroom, and found her purse by the bedside. She reached in and pulled out her phone, and forcefully punched in Paula's number.

"Sorry to call so early. I know you like to sleep in." She held the phone away from her ear so Paula could get past the initial discharge of profanity. "I know, and I'm sorry. I'm going to be sleeping there over this weekend, so if you could clear your stuff off my bed, I'd appreciate it." Again, the phone was held out. "It's still my room." A pause. "No you don't. I'm still paying my fees for that space so it's still mine." Jill rolled her eyes as she motioned Mike to come closer so he could hear the tirade. "My parents are arriving tonight, so I'll be coming back. I need closet space as well. If you have a problem with it, I'll let Karen know." She hung up.

"Who is Karen?" Mike never heard that name before.

"She's the Resident Assistant. She's was cool with what I was doing. And she knows that Paula has made my life difficult for the past year and a half anyway." Jill leaned up against the back of the couch.

"You wait.

Paula will take a few minutes and think it through, and then she'll call me back. Watch."

"Okay, so in the meantime, wanna help me put the rest of this food away?" They both had forgotten to put the groceries away. The last time that happened, it wasn't because of a disagreement. It was because they got a little too wrapped up in each other and ended up in the bedroom. Three hours later they had come out to find the ice cream melted all over the counter, the milk warm, and the chicken was already starting to smell bad. That's what happens when you can't afford to run the air conditioner in the middle of July.

Just as they closed the refrigerator for the last time and folded the last bag, Jill's phone rang. She had left it on the couch so she sprinted past Mike to grab it before it went to that awful voice mail message.

"Hello?" Jill didn't even notice who was on the line. She just wanted to catch the call.

"I'll be out of here for the whole weekend.

I'll shove all my stuff into my closet. Click"

Jill slowly moved the phone away from her ear, shaking her head. "I have not yet figured out if it's me or if she's just a bitch."

Mike would normally ask what happened but he hated getting Jill going on Paula. Besides, there was a lot more to get done to pull off this deception. "As long as we're all set. Let's get some of your clothes and you old science books together, run over there and get set up."

"I love you Mike."

"I know."

* * * * *

"I never felt so trapped before… I never felt so down… Going through the motions… dancing as if a sad clown…." Jill sang into the phone and then waited for a response.

"Erupting inside, wanting to flee… Until someone I love told me…. To let your heart be free…."

"Hi Daddio!" Jill wasn't sure if Arnie was even going to respond. It had to have been over ten years since they sang that song together.

"Hi there Bean, how are you?" Arnie and Doris had checked in to the Hyatt near campus and were freshening up. "We thought we'd come over to the dorm, see your room, and then take you out to dinner. Mom wants to take a rest for a little. You know how uptight she gets when she travels."

"That's okay, Dad." She hesitated. She was actually afraid to ask about bringing Mike along.

"Um, Dad?"

"What honey?" Arnie waited through the long pause, wondering what the 'um' meant. His little girl wasn't often the type to hesitate to speak out.

"I met a guy. I've kind of been seeing him for a while." Jill got the first part out with relative ease. It was the next part that terrified her, but before she could get the question out, Arnie relieved her angst.

"So, bring him along. We'd like to meet him."

Jill put her hand over the phone. "Well, you're getting your wish. You get to meet Dr. and Mrs. Arnold Kelly." She cleared her throat and then spoke back softly into the phone. "I'll find out if he's available. He's a sax player and he may have a gig tonight." By doing this, Jill thought she'd take some of the heat off. Mike could be a musician on the side, like her Daddio.

"Ah, a sax player. Looking forward to meeting him. And if he can't make dinner, maybe we can go see him play later."

Unnerved, Jill jumped on this.

"No, I don't think so. I have some studying to do tonight."

"Who said you had to come." Arnie was half joking, but Jill knew going to a jazz club was something he would really enjoy. She just couldn't be seen there with him, or it would blow her cover. She knew Mike was available tonight… just not tomorrow night. In fact, they still have to find a stand in for her, because she is still booked for tomorrow night, too.

"We'll figure it out. Meantime, let me get back to the books and we'll see you here at about 5:30, okay?" Jill was trying as hard as she could to project a blasé attitude while telling just one more lie.

"Perfect. Love you Bean."

Jill hung up and turned to Mike. "I need to take some kind of sedative. I'm really shaking inside." She didn't want to make eye contact with him, because she knew that being in the program, he was against her dealing with things with chemicals. "Just a half of a Xanax. You know, I'm not an addict. I barely drink, and don't do any illegal drugs."

"Hey, you don't have to justify anything to me. I didn't say a word." Mike went a bit further. "When I say the stuff I do, I am talking only about me, not you. Only you can determine if this is a problem for you."

"It's not."

* * * * *

"So how long have you been playing the saxophone?" Arnie asked the question as he shoveled another forkful of Caesar salad into his mouth.

"I've been playing since the sax was bigger than me, actually." Mike smiled. "Everyone in my family plays at least three instruments. Our living room was more like an orchestra pit." Mike reached for a piece of bread. "I just fell in love listening to Coltrane, and then later Michael Brecker."

"Love jazz. I was, in my day, a folk musician though." Arnie was now scraping the plate with his fork. "I used to play a little guitar and keyboard. In fact, Jilly Bean here used to sing with me. Did she ever tell you that?"

Mike knew he had to tread carefully here.

"Yeah, she mentioned she used to sing a little with you. She has a nice voice."

Jill stared down at the napkin on her lap through this conversation.

She didn't trust herself to participate. As good as she has become at her flurry of falsehoods, she knew that her father was still very good at reading her.

"So, is this going to be a career or are you majoring in something else?" Arnie asked the question, hoping that he wasn't digging too deep. He didn't want the evening to end with a "Bean Barrage." Jill, he knew, could be very sensitive when it came to her personal life.

Mike took a quick glance at Jill, who was still looking downward. "Still kind of up in the air. I haven't declared a major yet."

"Wait, but didn't Jill say you were a year ahead of her?" Arnie fully expected this young man to be already focused on something. His kids knew what they wanted and were already on a track while still in high school.

"I'm technically still a sophomore credit wise, sir. I had to take a semester off during my first year due to a medical issue." Mike was willing to be honest about everything, except his addiction problem, at least for now. It wouldn't go over well with this man if his first impression of his daughter's boyfriend were that he was a crack addict.

"Ah, I see." Arnie accepted this readily.

"And you are well now?" "Absolutely."

With salad plates cleared, the server brought the main course. Three fish platters and a big fat steak which was placed in front of Arnie.

"Dad, why are you still eating all that fatty red meat?" Jill never understood why her father, a renowned cardiologist, could do everything wrong regarding his own health, but was a sought-after speaker and consultant on heart health and the technique he had perfected.

"Very simple, my sweet." Arnie picked up his knife and fork. "Your mother never brings red meat in the house. I have it perhaps once every six months." He let out a sinister laugh and added,

"Tonight's the night!

Chapter 8

"So that song you always sing back and forth with your Dad on the phone… what is that?" Mike was curious. He hadn't heard it before he met Jill. He liked it.

"Oh that's just one from that album my dad used to play all the time by that obscure group he liked… I told you, Paradox Lost."

Mike was sitting at the sound board in the campus studio, mixing a recording of the song they had been working on. They had finally recorded it. "What if we tried to record it with a jazz lilt? Where can we find it to see if there's still a copyright on it?

"I have no idea. I don't even know if Dad still has the album, it's been so long." Jill was more interested in the song Mike was working on now. It was that heartbeat song. Jill was sure she could sell it to someone. Originally, she was thinking Cia, but now she wanted to consider Lady Gaga. In fact, what she really wanted was to release it herself. She had absolutely no chance of marketing it herself. She knew that, but it had such special meaning to her.

"Look, there's not really a rush. Graduation isn't for a few months. But if you are going to move with the songs we already have down, we need to come up with three or four more.

I just thought that would be cool to have that on your first album, kind of as a tribute to your Dad."

Jill cringed. *He just doesn't get it. This ruse has to go on until I'm at least making a living with music.* "Mike, listen. I can't put that on an album until I can pay my own way in this world. I need Dad to be helping me with my supposed Med School money.

That's the only way I can survive trying to break into music and not go hungry."

Mike got suddenly cold and unresponsive.

He spun around on the studio chair and bent over, fiddling with a sax case on the floor. He didn't need anything from it, but he wasn't as good as throwing her off as Jill was at diverting him.

"Whatever," he whispered.

Jill wasn't backing down. She needed Mike personally and professionally. He not only had the contacts in New York and all over the music industry, but she had fallen for him deeply and completely. Until right now, she had been able to look past this rigorous honesty to which he was so firmly adhering. She could feel her pulse pounding in her neck. Everything would be on the line if she didn't pick her words carefully.

"Mike, you know I love you. I want us to continue this journey together, but it has to, for the time being, be on my terms." She paused to see if he would react, but he remained bent over the equipment with his back to her.

"I don't want to succeed in music because I'm attached to you. I want to know I can make it on my own."

Mike spun around.

"If you want to, as you put it, make it on your own, then how can you continue to lie to your parents, taking their money on false pretenses, and ask me to perpetuate your lies, all in the name of your authenticity. You're full of crap!" He jumped up, grabbed his bag and lurched for the door of the studio.

Jill's legs turned to spaghetti. She had never seen her soft-spoken, sweet Michael be so reactive and show such venom. "Wait, Mike. Please. Don't go."

"I can't talk to you right now. I'm angry and I don't trust my words." He was gone.

As the door slammed behind him, Jill was left in the sound-proof studio. She was half crying and half laughing. Laughing because she knew she could scream out in agony and nobody would hear her, and crying because she may just have ruined the best thing that ever happened to her.

She slumped down into a ball against the back of the door, resting her head on her crossed arms and wept.

* * * * *

What seemed like a few minutes turned into several hours. Jill had cried herself to sleep, but was suddenly awakened when someone attempted to open the studio door. The lights had been on a timer and had gone out almost two hours prior. She jumped up, and as the door opened, the lights began to come on once again.

Naomi pushed the door open further, to find Jill swollen eyed and groggy.

"Hey girl, you okay?"

"Yeah, sure." Jill stretched her back.

"I just fell asleep.

"Been burning the candle, you know." She fumbled to look for her phone. "Oh shit. I must have been out for a while. I'm late for ensemble practice." She was still woozy and glanced around the studio, trying to get her head straight. Spotting her back pack, she endeavored to sound matter-of-fact. "You cutting something or just laying down some tracks?"

"I'm doing another audition for another incoming." Naomi was making a name for herself as a classical pianist, and was also making a nice living doing these audition recordings for Jacobs's hopefuls. "It hasn't gotten old yet, as long as they're paying me." She looked over Jill's shoulder who was now at the exit door. "This one's late.

They can never find the studio. What have you been up to?"

"Can I call you later? I am so late; they're probably going to kick me out of ensemble." Jill really didn't care much for Naomi, a carry over, she figured, from the days when she was with Mike doing the drugs. "I can't afford to be late again. I mean I know they need more mezzo-soprano voices, and they can't afford to lose mine right now, but I am really pushing it." She grabbed her bag and pulled open the door. "I talk to you later."

* * * * *

Jill had bundled up substantially, but February was exceptionally cold on campus. She wasn't sure she should even go home or find some place to hang out for a few hours. Ensemble rehearsal was usually uplifting for her, but for some reason, this time it wasn't enough to take her mind off of Mike and the words they had had that morning.

Her heart was heavy, and the wind was whipping around her neck sending a chill down her back. Her fuzzy boots were barely doing their job of keeping her feet warm.

80

I'd rather be at home, in bed, in his arms. I don't even know if I should call him or wait for him to call me.

As she approached the Student Center, she thought she saw him entering from the West Side. She called, "Mike!" He either didn't hear her or was just ignoring her.

Am I pushing him too far? Have I asked him to do too much that goes against his better judgment? It's not him that's lying, it's me. He's such a sissy. A goodie-goodie.

She approached the South Side Door, tried to open it but it was locked. *Damn it, why do they always forget to open all sides?* She knocked on the door, and tried to motion someone over to open the door. After two or three minutes, she finally had some success.

"Thanks," she said as she shivered.

Jill left all of her coats, scarves and sweaters on as she navigated her way to the cafeteria. She glanced around to see if she could spot Mike, to no avail. Maybe it wasn't him.

Maybe she saw someone who looked like him, instead. She turned on her heels and headed back towards the West Side door.

Figuring on the fact that the apartment was as much hers as it was his, she didn't want the anger to fester any longer than it had already. Mike had a tendency to use emotions as an excuse to escape and she did not want him to use all of this as a reason to use or drink anything. The more she thought about it the faster she found herself walking. There was still some residue of ice and snow on the side of the walkways from the last snow storm, although as she looked up, the skies looked rather ominous, as if they were as angry as Mike. She wanted to get home before anything started to fall from above. She already felt as if she had the weight of the world on her shoulders.

Jill knew all of the short cuts Mike had shown her, but that didn't make the trip seem any shorter on foot. She knew Mike had nothing on the schedule for today. In fact, she was planning on cooking at home now that the landlord finally replaced the oven. She was almost running now. Her backpack was bouncing against her back, but she barely noticed how hard it was hitting her. She reached the walk-up, letting the pack slip off one shoulder to fish out her keys just as her phone rang.

Dropping the pack on the ground, thankfully right next to a pile of yellow snow, she slipped her gloved hand into the partially unzipped side fishing around for her phone. "Hello?"

She knew it was Mike, because she had set another one of her distinctive ring tones just for him, but she played dumb anyway.

"Hey babe, are you okay?" Mike spoke gently again.

"Yeah, I'm just outside. I had ensemble practice." She neglected to mention that she had cried herself to sleep in the studio and was there for hours, late for rehearsal.

"That I knew." Mike had already gotten a call from Naomi. "Was just wondering what happened after I left you. Your practice wasn't until…." His voice trailed off. He was treading into dangerous territory. "This is ridiculous. Come inside. We're ten feet apart and talking on the phone!"

"You're right. This is silly. Bye." She tried to smile through her voice. Mike was blessed (or cursed) with the talent of being able to tell people's moods over the phone, so Jill had to be really careful when she called him not to let on how she REALLY was.

The door of the building seemed heavier than usual. Pulling it open, Jill caught it with her foot and bent over to pick up her pack. Regaining her balance, she walked in and the door slammed shut behind her, startling her.

Guess I'm more nervous about this than I thought.

Mike was waiting with the door open, and a cup of cocoa in his hand. He reached for her pack, and traded her: his cup of cocoa for her pack. She walked by him, accepting the terms of the deal, placing the cup precariously on the side of the dining room table and began to unpeel the layers of clothing.

"I'm sorry, I should have called."

Mike was already in the kitchen making another cup of cocoa for himself. "I was pretty angry when I left, and I know we were both kind of upset. I just thought you might come home before rehearsal, that's all."

"I was upset," she began.

"I needed some time to think." After a few seconds of silence, because she knew it was her that needed to clarify things, she continued. "Look, Mike. I know how you feel about all of this. And I don't want to continue to put you into positions that make you so uncomfortable.

What you said made sense… if you are on the outside, looking in. But I fully expect to parlay this unbelievable education I'm getting into an explosive and lucrative career. The vocal training, though classical, is making my voice, my control, my range… all of it… so much better."

She studied him intently. He was clearly waiting for more. "I anticipate being able to give them back every penny they've given to me. I think I know them pretty well. They'll forgive the lies, if I can show them I can make my own way, be successful and all that."

"Yeah, Jill, but at what cost?" Mike had come from a family that kept no secrets. Even when he was screwed up with the drugs, his parents knew. Not only did they know, but they were an active part of his recovery. He is not only rigorously honest, but sometimes brutally so. "Doesn't it keep you up at night knowing that you're lying to your mom and dad? I mean, where is your conscience? Didn't they teach you not to lie to them?" Mike was stirring his cocoa as he came in and sat down at the table.

Jill sat down opposite him. "If you had been around my house during my high school years and even into the first year of college, you would have understood. My dad, for some unknown reason, absolutely refused to finance a music education.

And that was after we used to play and sing all the time together. I mean, I know it wasn't because he didn't think I had talent. I still can't figure it out."

Mike was watching Jill intently. There were times that even when she was just talking, he heard singing. The sound of her voice mesmerized him. He knew when he left her at the studio that he would give in because he loved her, and didn't want to lose her. He hadn't heard a word she said once he sat down at the table and began staring into her eyes.

"Okay." He didn't know what he was giving into. "I will abide by your decision not to tell them. Yet. But listen, I want you to consider it soon." All of sudden a compromise popped into his head. "How about this? How about let's go over to New York on spring break and do some auditioning." He wasn't sure where he was going with this.

"Maybe see if there's a back-up spot for a group open or a shot at a club gig."

"I have to be here to graduate. I absolutely have to finish and get a degree here."

"Why? I'm not." Mike had dropped out and was earning a living as a regular at Buddy's club and playing gigs in and around Bloomington and other small towns in Indiana.

"Remember, I have to pull off graduation and getting into med school in New York to keep this thing going." Jill was going to let Mike get away with this one. He's very anxious to get up to New York and ply his craft, and he's only here because of her.

"Oh yeah, okay."

Mike had just agreed to do what was necessary. He was putting his music career on a back burner. It was only another three or four months. "Besides, with your studio pass I can get a lot done while we're still here."

Their conversation was interrupted by Arnie's familiar ringtone. Jill rooted through her purse, slid her finger over the screen and sang, "I never felt so trapped before… I never felt so down… Going through the motions… dancing as if a sad clown…." and then waited for his usual response

"Hi Daddio!" Jill decided to start this call on an upbeat, fully expecting the barrage of questions, but most of Arnie's conversation was centered on things at home. He sounded really content to her, so she decided this was a perfect opportunity to drop the one bomb that she would really have to defend. "So, Dad, I've made my decision."

There was absolute silence at the other end of the line. Jill knew he would be unhappy with her decision, and fight for his alma mater.

Geez, it isn't even football season. "It's partly professional and partly personal, but it satisfies all of my needs." Again, silence.

"There are a few things I need to tell you. Please hear me out before you react, okay." Arnie had a habit of blowing up before he heard the whole story, and if he didn't do that, he would be so busy thinking about what he wanted to say, he wouldn't hear the whole story in the first place.

"Well, you have my attention."

"First," Jill began softly, assuming she needed to save her passion and emotion for the argument that would surely ensue. "Since Eric is already at UNC Medical and planning on a career in Cardiology..."

Jill drifted off, fully expecting to be interrupted, but Arnie was still silent.

He's actually listening to me.

"I've decided that I would rather go into Obstetrics and Gynecology."

She let out the rest of her breath into the phone, for dramatic effect.

"Okay, that sounds like a reasonable decision." Arnie sounded to Jill as if he were sedated.

"Dad, are you feeling, okay?" She was half kidding, half serious. "I thought you were hell bent on me going into cardio and taking over your practice back at home."

"This is your life, Bean." Arnie was very calm. "Eric and I have been talking about this, and he has already committed to doing that. He is actually going to study cardio-thoracic surgery, and has intentions of really taking the practice into broader dimensions."

"Okay, that's great, Dad." *Phew!* Jill was not sure the legacy shit was going to go over so easily. She was right.

"What do you mean you're not going to UNC? Every Kelly has studied medicine there for three generations. What the...." Arnie was dumbfounded. This was a done deal, as far as he thought. He never even bothered to follow up on her application, once he was sure she marked the legacy box and knew her MCAT scores and GPA. "Jill Kelly, you are absolutely going to UNC."

"Dad, you didn't even let me finish." Jill felt that familiar lump in her throat.

Her father was very good at evoking her anxiety and bringing her to tears. He was the only one in the world who could push her buttons so easily.

"Dad, I have a very good reason for my decision."

"What the hell could be a better reason than family tradition... legacy... all of our family's hopes for you?" He was pulling out all the stops.

I'm not backing down. I'm using my best shot right now.

"I'm in love."

Mike froze in the doorway on his way back from the bedroom. He had given Jill some privacy, but heard her voice getting louder and louder.

He mouthed the words back to her with a questioning look on his face:

'you're in love?'

Nodding her head towards Mike, she continued her conversation.

"Dad, I got accepted to SUNY, and I'm going up to New York. Mike and I are going to look for a place together. He already has steady work up there."

The pulse in her neck was disrupting her speech and her breathing, but she forged forward.

Arnie threw a barrage of questions. He was disappointed in her decision not to follow family tradition at UNC, but was trying to keep an open mind. "I'll have to look and see who I know up there.

When is your graduation?

Are you planning on just living together or are you getting married?

Will you consider an internship or residency down here?

Are you going to plan on staying up there forever?"

Arnie didn't give her a chance to answer.

"If you're getting married, are you going to settle up there, raise a family in the city?"

"No wedding plans, no, not yet.   There are plenty of internship opportunities in the city."

She rolled her eyes.

"Come on, Dad, you know that. New York is one of the best places to be for me."

"Let me think on this." Arnie was not convinced, but at least Jill had started the process.

They finished up the conversation cordially, but not the way she had hoped.

"Okay Dad, please give Mom my love." She pressed the red button on her phone and then dropped it back in her purse. Her head dropped forward, her chin nearly resting on her chest.

While she was on the phone, Mike had fixed her a second cup of coca. Jill smiled, but was still shivering both from the phone conversation and from her walk back from the Student Center.

"I have an idea. While the cocoa was very helpful, is there any way you can think of that would warm me up and make me feel a little better?"

"Subtle, kid." Mike jumped up, took Jill by hand and led her back to the bedroom.

Chapter 9

"Hey Mike, did you know you could buy tassels on line?" Jill scrolled through the website methodically. It was four in the morning but her angst over surviving the next several weeks had been costing her sleep, normal eating habits and her sanity. Mike was on a tear with his saxophone and had been commuting back and forth from New York, having gotten a great gig at an inventive and well known jazz club just outside of Manhattan. He was playing every weekend, and coming home during the week, so he hadn't been much help to Jill as she tried to put together the next canyon she would have to cross.

She swiveled around in the chair to find Mike out cold. He had fallen off to sleep after a particularly zealous romp.

He always gets that way when he comes home from the city. I know the feeling, though. There is nothing more exhilarating than hitting the notes to an appreciative audience... to having them groove to an original song... to getting lost in the melody and have that warm feeling descend upon you when you blend the harmony of your soul and spirit in song with the melody of a love song someone wrote FOR YOU.

Jill didn't blame him for falling asleep. She was still a little winded herself.

She thought back to the first time they made love, on the day she got accepted into Jacobs. She hadn't even given it a thought that she gave her virginity to this man. She wasn't planning on waiting until she got married or anything, but she didn't expect it to be a matter-of-fact occurrence that took a back seat to something else in her life. *Everything seems to have taken a back seat to my mission,* she thought.

She turned back to the screen, trying to recall what the exact color was that she needed to order for the degree she was "earning." She toggled back to the Indiana University webpage to see if there was any information on it about the tassels. She found nothing. She jotted down a couple of names and phone numbers listed on the Biology Department's page, and then tried to remember a few of her classmates from freshman year with whom she was in class for some of the underclassmen required classes that first semester.

Paula took that same class. Shit, she'll be no help. I better just get some sleep.

The muted light from the screensaver cast just enough of a subdued shadow when she turned the bathroom light off for her to find her way to her side of the bed. Mike had rolled over onto his back, and had positioned himself in the middle of the cramped full sized bed. Jill tried to gently nudge him enough to slip the corner of her pillow out from under his head without waking him, but when she did, he let out a soft moan,

"Not now, Naomi."

Jill yanked the pillow out and hit him in the head.

"I hope that's just another one of those drug dreams!"

"Wha.. Wha.. Hey what'd you do that for?"

Mike roused himself, making out Jill's silhouette now that the screen had gone almost completely dark. "What are you doing up still?

"What are you dreaming about?" Jill had her hands on her hips, and was ready for confrontation.

"I have no idea." Mike did, however, notice his erection, so drawing his knees up and pulling the blanket toward him he carefully asked, "Why?"

"You were moaning Naomi's name again.

Was she with you in New York?" Jill was letting the unattractive, jealous side out that she knew was a probably going to escalate the 'discussion.'

"You know she's up there already." He started out slowly, trying to draw attention to his face and away from his lower body.

"Honey, you know I haven't seen her since she left last year."

Mike was trying to figure out first why he would have said her name, and second why Jill was so irritable. "It probably was another 'drug dream' and you know she was in my life then."

Jill sat down on the edge of the bed. With her hands at her face, she gently wept,

"I'm sorry.

I know all of that." She hated when she cried. In her thinking that was a sign of weakness. After a long pause, she continued. "I guess I'm just a little uptight about the next step in the process.

My folks AND my brothers are coming in for graduation, and I'm not exactly sure how I'm going to pull this off." She reached over to the nightstand and grabbed the last tissue from the box, dabbing her eyes and the softly blowing her nose.

"We'll figure it all out, Jill. But not at four in the morning."

Mike was exhausted, having travelled in from New York after a Sunday evening session that ran until ten, a race to the airport to catch the plane, a turbulent flight and coming home to his Jelly Bean.

"I love you and whatever it takes, we'll figure it out. Now come here."

Jill pulled down the blanket on her side of the bed while Mike slithered over to his. She slipped into the bed and nestled herself under his arm. There was that familiar sound.

BUM bum BUM bum BUM bum. She believed at that moment, that she would never get tired of hearing it, and that someday, that sound would make her famous.

* * * * *

Both of them forgot to close the blinds on the bedroom window, and the morning sun was unrelenting. Jill had only slept for two hours before she heard the sound of those damn birds outside.

What did he say they were? Kentucky Warblers? They can go back to their old Kentucky home as far as I'm concerned.

Jill threw back what was left of the blanket and swung her legs over the side of the bed. Mike hadn't moved. She used the palms of her hands, rubbing her eyes trying to awaken to what would be a jam-packed day. Mondays always were, but today there were two choral group performances at the student center on top of two finals.

Jill stood up lazily, and lumbered toward the bathroom, picking up her bathrobe and a pair of clean underwear and bra from the laundry basket on her way.

Damn, I meant to put all that stuff away before he got home.

The shower always steamed up the tiny bathroom they share in their apartment. According to Mike, if they were moving to New York and wanted to rent an apartment there, it would be a lot smaller than this, and the commute would be substantial. Jill, having been living in small cities and towns all her life couldn't relate to the cost of living in Manhattan.

This was why I have to keep this going. I know I'm going to break into this fast and furious, but until I do, Dr. Kelly is going to have to help whether he knows it or not.

Jill let the hot water pour down the back of her neck as she did her shoulder rolls and sang a few scales.

Am I that vain or does it really sound that good in the shower?

The sound of her voice echoed long after the thought went out of her head.

"You almost done in there?"

Mike's voice was always scratchy in the morning, especially after he had played a gig.

"The coffee's ready."

"What time is it?"

Jill toweled off quickly and roughly. She loved the feel of her blood pumping up to the surface of her skin to get her awake in the morning.

The only thing better would have been a good orgasm.

Mike wasn't a fan of morning sex. Always self-conscious about his breath and being unshaven. She was out of the bathroom and dressed in five minutes, coffee mug in hand and the newspaper open, on the table.

"I think you're the only one I know who still reads the paper."

Mike was a web-surfer, getting most of his news from websites and television.

He only really read about pop culture to see if there was any news dirt on musicians he knew, or any gigs he should see, or know about. "Anything important happening in the world today?"

Jill grunted. She turned the page and reached for her coffee, as if she hadn't heard him. Focus was a strong suit for her. She had learned to be able to live two separate lives a long time ago, and was able to maintain them individually. That took a great deal of concentration, as did the separate lives that she lived within each life. Here she was, getting a degree in voice, with a concentration in Operatic Soprano and a minor in music theory, while she has been singing soft jazz and some folk and alternative rock to make a living on the weekends. All the while she was convincing her other life participants that she was getting her degree in Microbiology.

Wait, did he say something? "Huh?"

"I asked if you knew I hit the lottery."

Mike smirked. "Nothing important. So where did that cute little head of yours take you?"

"Oh, I was just thinking about the day ahead," she lied again.

"Do you happen to know what color tassel they get in the B.S. Degree in Biology? I need to get a hold of one."

"I have no idea."

Mike looked puzzled, but only for a second. He knew she had those wheels spinning again, ready to hatch another plan.

"You remind me of Lucy."

"Lucy who?"

"Didn't you ever watch the old "I Love Lucy" reruns with Lucille Ball and Desi Arnaz?"

Mike seemed genuinely surprised by Jill's lack of recognition when he started to tell her.

"You know, the series from the fifties and sixties, and Lucy's best friend was Ethel.

They were always getting themselves into scrapes because of Lucy's plots and plans and brilliant ideas?"

Slowly Mike began to realize that she wasn't hearing a word he was saying.

"Jill?"

"Oh yeah, I remember." Lip service.

"So do you know anyone that was pre-Med or pre-Dental or something along those lines?"

"JILL!"

He made a small fist and knocked on her head gently.

"Hello?"

Shaking her head, Jill realized she was in another dimension. She really wasn't hearing him or even remotely connected to anything that was happening at the moment.

"I'm sorry.

You know what?

I'm so tired. I'm going to blow off my morning class.

It's a review for Wednesday's final and even if I fail the test, I'll get a B." Jill stood up and turned toward Mike.

"I'm going to go back to bed for a couple of hours. I'm setting the clock, but will you wake me by 9:30?"

"I'll have to call you. I'm running over to have coffee with Buddy at 9:00.

He wants to run something by me." Mike kissed Jill on the forehead, and picked up a tote bag full of folders. He started for the front door but stopped and turned back.

"Put the phone on the night stand and make sure the ringer is on. Love you, baby."

He was gone. Jill sauntered back into the bedroom, and without taking her clothes off, collapsed into the bed. Everything that had been so critical in her mind was gone. Sleep. Sweet, uninterrupted sleep. That's all she wanted.

* * * * *

Okay, so now I have to change his ringtone too. Wild thing is not the easiest song to wake up to when you're in a deep sleep.

Jill opened one eye and tried to make out the glowing red numbers on her alarm clock. It read 9:25. She had wondered why Mike called and the alarm hadn't gone off. A minute later, Wild Thing started screaming at her again.

"Why didn't you pick up the phone? Were you in the bathroom or something?"

"I didn't get to it fast enough. My clock hadn't gone off and I was too groggy." Sitting on the edge of the bed again, Jill thought she wouldn't be able to get a clear head at all this time. "Let me go and get my act together.

This test is at 10:00 and I need to eat something, too."

"Okay, good luck."

"Not to worry. This is an oral. I'll nail it. Easy piece. In fact, it turns out it's my audition piece." She thought back to the day she recorded that song. She took an unbelievable chance sending in such an Avant Garde arrangement of an operatic solo. Nobody ever said anything to her about it. She had even had some instructors who served on the admissions committee. Not one person ever mentioned how different her approach was. Perhaps that was the key.

She hung up the phone, picked up her purse, stopped in the kitchen and grabbed a bottle of water from the refrigerator and a granola bar from the pantry and was out the door.

Save those damn songbirds, Jill loved the springtime in Indiana. Between the black cherry trees in bloom and those magnificent dogwoods, it looked and smelled beautiful to walk around campus and in parks. Whatever she had been allergic to at home in North Carolina didn't seem to bother her in the springtime the entire four years in college. Jill couldn't help wondering what New York would bring. She walked across campus sipping on her water and running through **Star Vicino** in her head. She had to stop and clear her throat several times.

Just morning phlegm. I'll be fine. She started from the beginning.

SHIT! She started again.

Before she realized it, Jill had arrived at the East Studio Building where the testing was going to occur. She hadn't had the chance to run through the whole piece. She wondered if they were going to do this alphabetically, randomly or first come. She stood outside of the building with her purse over one shoulder, and held one finger to her right ear. Somehow, she found it comforting to do that, as it reminded her of being in the recording studio where she had no fear. She heard better, she seemed to think, with her left ear.

"Everyone please take a seat. Shhhhhhhhh." Patricia Stiles stood in front of thirty-two anxious voice students. She was an accomplished soprano, but Jill had a few run-ins with her on those Monday mornings when she dragged herself into class late. She knew she would pass the class, but she also knew Ms. Stiles would be hard on her.

"A basket is going around the room," she began.

"As it comes to you, please take ONE piece of paper. On that paper is a number.

THAT is the order in which you will perform this morning." She paused.

"Do I need to repeat the instructions?"

The room, with a collective conscious, shook their heads back and forth, gently. Nobody wanted her to repeat it, as that would mean frustration on her part, and NOBODY wanted Ms. Stiles aggravated before she graded them.

Jill bowed her head as if in prayer, when she realized she had picked the number one.

Well, at least I can get it over with, and there's little chance of her getting angry that early.

She ran through the words but now she couldn't remember the melody. She kept hearing Mike's smooth jazz riffs in between the classical piano plinking of Naomi.

NAOMI. Why was he dreaming about Naomi.

She shook her head and rolled her shoulders to try to relax.

Don't go back there, Bean.

Jill's heart was pounding in her chest. She was alarmed because being nervous about performing wasn't typical for her.

And why all of a sudden 'Bean'. Only Daddy calls me that. Why is he creeping in? I must be having a guilty conscience.

Jill didn't even hear it. She was so lost in her own thoughts that she didn't hear Ms. Stiles begin the exam by calling the first number, which, of course, was her. She was already on to number three.

Apparently, nobody had picked number two and I guess she thinks nobody picked number one either. So now what do I do?

She opened the paper again, and realizing that it was handwritten, she reached down into her purse and fumbled around until she found a black ball point pen, to match the original ink.

I could lose everything doing this.

While number three was performing, Jill carefully drew another one next to the one already there, and began praying that nobody answered when it was number eleven's turn.

If they do, I'll deal with it then.
"So, we're at number 10 and we've already had three people who haven't shown up. Please know people, that there were exactly thirty-two slips of paper in that basket. So, if someone skipped the test, that's on them.

If you're late, you don't get a number." Ms. Stiles looked straight at Jill. She continued. "If two claim to have the same number, then we REALLY have a problem. Okay, number 10."

As the student who was singing was reaching the end, Jill was on the edge of her chair, with her purse stowed, and her water ready to take one last sip. SHE was going to be number eleven, no matter what.

"Numbers three through ten may be excused, and we will be taking a ten minute intermission." Ms. Stiles rifled through some papers, sat down and began making notes on a few of the papers. Jill sat frozen. She fought with herself.

How have I stooped so low? When did I become so manipulative? Is all of this worth sacrificing my soul?

The pounding in her head was relentless. Her heartbeat was resounding throughout her body so much that she could feel it in her fingers.

Should I tell her the truth up front or should I try to pull this off? If I get caught, I don't graduate. If she fails me on the final, I get a C in voice. Who cares? I got the training. That's all that matters. I can't live with the guilt.

She glanced over at her instructor. Ms. Stiles was intently reviewing her papers.

If I interrupt her, she'll be pissed off. I have to take my chances. What was that expression Mike was talking about... Integrity is what you do when nobody is watching...

Jill slowly rose, holding on to her water bottle as if it were the last sustenance she would ever see. She gradually made her way down the aisle, and as she neared her instructor, Ms. Stiles suddenly looked up. "I had a feeling I'd be seeing you up here."

Jill hung her head. "Ms. Stiles, I must tell you. I had number one. I was so lost in thought, running the music through my head and thinking about too many things, that I didn't hear you begin. I decided that I would rather you fail me on this oral exam than try to cheat my way through it. I have enough issues going on in my life that I can't seem to reconcile. I don't want to add guilt to the list. If you want me to leave now, I will." She picked up her head, and for the first time in two months, actually made eye contact with the woman who taught her so much, but made her feel so small.

"Thank you."

Ms. Stiles almost smiled. Jill's first thought was that she would never give her the satisfaction of a smile. She waited for the rest of the response.

"Please be seated. You may sing last."

Jill's heart dropped from her throat to her abdomen. Her shoulders followed. She fought it, but the tears started to pool up in the corners of her eyes.

"Thank you, Ms. Stiles."

She decided the less said right now the better. Jill turned on her heels and almost ran back up the aisle. Her heart was no longer pounding as hard, but still beating very fast.

She was dizzy and light headed, and barely made it to her seat. Collapsing into a heap, she listened very carefully to every single degree candidate sing their final exam piece, clapping, assessing, and comparing. Gradually she felt much better. About Ms. Stiles, about herself, about everything.

* * * * *

"Mike?" Her hand was shaking as she tried to hold the phone to her ear. "I almost blew the whole thing, but ultimately nailed it. I'll tell you what happened tonight." She was trying to have this conversation on the way to her second exam, one in Music Theory, which was something she hadn't even cracked a book for all semester. She loved the class. Every time the professor opened his mouth in class, her mind became that old familiar sponge. She could practically teach the class.

"I'll be home around six."

The class was given ninety minutes to take the exam and Jill completed it effortlessly within the first thirty minutes. She glanced over what she had done, and confident that there wasn't anything incomplete or incorrect, she jumped up, dropped the papers off in the box on the desk in the front, and left.

No problem. I gotta get something to eat and then get over to the Student Center Auditorium.

Practically skipping across campus, Jill spotted her old roommate, standing outside Simon Hall. "Hey, Paula!" Jill shouted. Paula spotted her but barely acknowledged her. Paula was still smoking, after giving Jill such shit about it when they were freshmen.

"I need to ask a favor of you."

Jill broke into a hard run. She was still in pretty good shape even though she had stopped distance running by the time she was a junior. It wasn't because she couldn't do it, but because she could never find the time to do it. It felt good to get her heart pumping for a good reason, for a change.

"What's up chickee?"

Jill hated that. Her name was Jill, or Jelly Bean. She really didn't like this girl, but she needed her. Paula took one more drag on her nearly crushed cigarette, and blew the smoke directly at Jill.

"I wonder if you know someone getting a degree in Biology. I just need to know what color tassel they get for a B.S. in Biology or Chemistry or one of those sciences." Jill knew Paula had switched her major right after she had moved out, but had no idea what she was studying. Paula was still very much a lone wolf kind of person. She didn't have very many friends if any at all. She went to class, she studied, and she worked at a part time menial job at the Student Center to keep her financial aid.

"Yeah, I do, as a matter of fact." Paula was being snippy. "Who wants to know?"

Me, dumbass.

"I do." Jill was trying to contain herself. "So what color is your tassel?

I assume you're graduating next month, right?" Jill stopped herself.

She didn't want to push too hard. Paula was never forthcoming with favors, even when it didn't demand much of her.

"Gold… and yes, I'm graduating."

Paula let out a snort. "I'm not doing the ceremony shit though."

"Why not?" Jill was almost afraid to hear the answer.

"Ain't nobody bothering to come up for it. I got accepted to Pharmacy School anyway, and I'm leaving next Tuesday."

"So can I ask a huge favor?"

Jill took a deep breath. This could go one way or the other.

"Can I pick up your tassel for you and then mail it to you wherever you're headed. I'd really like to do that for you."

"What are you up to?"

Paula has seen this before. Jill was always pulling this kind of shit.

"Who are you going to lie to this time?"

"It's not a total lie."

Do I tell her the whole story? "I just need to borrow it for an hour."

"I don't care. You'll need my I.D. to pick it up. Just tell 'em you're my roommate, which you still are, by the way." Paula sneered. Jill thought to herself that maybe all this time had passed and she never really knew Paula, and what motivated her.

Sad that nobody was coming to see her graduate.

"Well, congratulations on graduate school. I'll come by next Monday, before you leave, to pick up your I.D."

"Fine." Paula lit another cigarette and walked away.

Chapter 10

Jill was once again awakened by the morning light careening in through the blinds and bouncing off the dresser mirror, landing directly on her face. Mike, once again, was unaffected. She thought back for a split second, how it used to do that in her bedroom at home, until she finally rearranged her furniture. Her life has been rearranged so much since then.

Jumping up out of bed, Jill knew this day was going to be one of her biggest challenges yet. Her parents and her brothers were all in town, planning on meeting Mike at the East Gate of Memorial Stadium, expecting to see her receive her undergraduate diploma, a Bachelor of Science in Microbiology. She took a quick shower, toweled off and had her clothes on before Mike had stirred even a little. She was in the kitchen getting the coffee started when she heard him groaning.

"You okay in there?"

"Just stretching."

Mike slept in the nude and had thrown the covers off. Rolling over the side, he called in to Jill.

"I'm taking a quick shower."

He tiptoed into the bathroom, still very shy about his body, and quietly closed the door behind him.

Better not do too much caffeine this morning. Jill slipped the newspaper out of its plastic bag and glanced at her watch. She slid the chair out from under the table, slithered into the seat, took a deep breath and tried to focus on anything but what was in her head.

Man, this charade is making me too old, too fast.

The vibration function of her phone kicked in, telling her that almost no time had passed since her watch read 7:20 am. It was set to remain silent until 8:00 Am., but there was that picture on the screen. Her Daddio. Why is he calling so early? The thing isn't until 10:00.

"Morning, Dad," Jill whispered, endeavoring to sound calm.

"What, no Paradox?"

Arnie was trying to hold his phone with his shoulder while he was trying unsuccessfully to tie his tie.

"I just wanted to check in with you before I fed the animals, prior to coming over to campus. Are you excited?"

"Mike is still asleep, so I was trying to be quiet. Actually Dad, I'm a little nervous. Or maybe I'm just excited. I don't know. I have butterflies, ya know?"

Jill knew exactly why she felt the way she did.

"Lay off the coffee. We'll meet you at the East Gate 9 after the ceremony and see about some lunch. Love you, Bean."

Believe it or not, "I love you too, Daddio."

* * * * *

Mike droves carefully through the back route to the West 1 entrance by the scoreboard. He seemed relieved to drop her. Her bouncing knees and incessant chatter was more than he could handle. It was going to be hard enough for him to perpetuate this farce at her request. Jill knew that, but she also knew she was the one that had to pull off the hard part. At least she was prepared. She leaned over to him and kissed him.

"You sure you have everything? Both tassels, both honor slips?"

Mike had tried to tell her not to try to get away with honors for the science degree, but she had voted him down. She insisted she needed the honors to be medical school material.

"Yup! I think I'm ready to rock and roll."

She spun around back at Mike.

"Did you hear that? I made a funny. Ya know my mother always used to tell me that the truest things are said in jest. We're going to look back on this and …."

"Jill, GO!"

Mike had to stop her. The car behind him was honking and the line for drop off was growing.

"Good luck. Love you, baby."

* * * * *

Jill pushed her way through the crowds around the red sign that said Jacobs School of Music. She decided that since the school is so big, and nobody's name was being called, she was going to sit with her friends and fellow graduates. I don't know anyone anymore is the sciences except Paula, and she isn't even here.

"Excuse me."

Her cap under her arm, Jill pushed her way through but didn't see the right sign.

"Does anyone know where Jacobs is?"

"Those nerds are way over on the other side. You came in the wrong gate, "came a voice from behind her. She turned around quickly, angered by being referred to as a nerd.

"Eric!

What are you doing back here?"

She threw her arms around her brother, and held him as if she were never going to see him again.

"Where are Mom and Dad?"

Suddenly she pushed him away and glanced anxiously around the sea of black and red.

"Relax. They're in their seats upstairs."

Eric always had a calming effect on his little sister.

"I wanted to come down and congratulate you on your degree, since I probably won't be able to give this to you later."

He reached inside the breast pocket of his blue sport coat, and pulled out a small box.

"What is it? What did you do?"

Jill hurriedly tore off the paper to find an aqua blue Tiffany box. "Eric..." She carefully opened the box, and inside was a sterling silver jelly bean, with a G-clef engraved on one side and the year 2017 on the other.

"Wow. Thank you so much."

Tiny little tears started to form in the outside corners of both of her eyes. Eric was the only one besides Mike that knew her heart, accepted and supported her, and would always be there for her, no matter what.

"Thank you."

"All Arts and Science graduates, please line up. No particular order necessary."

A deep, resonant voice came booming through a bull horn.

"As per your instructions, you need only sit with like colored tassels."

"So, if are you staying here, you better lose the music tassel."

Eric had proven to Jill that he didn't want to be around if things started to crumble for her. Not today, anyway.

"Let me hold on to it for safe keeping. I better get back up to the seats." He started to walk away, but called back to her.

"Hey, am I going to get to meet this Mike guy?"

"Yup.

Mom and Dad have been in touch with him. They're supposed to be saving a seat for him." Jill's face was pink with an unnatural blush. She really wanted Eric to like Mike. That would make everything in her world just about perfect.

"Eric, please… don't try to scare him off with a baseball bat or anything like that, like you and Ivan did to all my high school dates. I really like him." She paused for a second.

"Eric? I think I love him."

Eric winked at her. "I won't be too hard on him. Can't speak for Ivan." He winked again and then he was gone.

Breathing a little easier because her biggest hurdle would be crossed by lunchtime, Jill got in line with a group of total strangers. She didn't care. This was it. If I can make it through this and get them on a plane tomorrow morning, I'm on my way.

The arena was humming with excitement. The intensity did not approach the flutter in Jill's stomach. The micro band was playing softly in the far corner yet she could feel the vibration in her head. People were milling about and Jill felt as if she were floating above, it all. Her mind raced, full of 'what ifs' and 'oh nos.' Light-headed and foggy in thought, she tried to focus on the program. Paul O'Neill, an Indiana University alumnus and former U.S. Treasury Secretary was the guest speaker.

That's nice.

Jill thumbed through the pages, trying to concentrate on the print, and glossing over the pictures. Suddenly a panic descended upon her. She started to cough and was choking on her own saliva, unable to catch her breath. Under the different colleges, her name…

it isn't in the right place in the undergraduate listings. Oh Geez. Mom is going to see that. Shit! She reads every last word of these things. Oh G-d Mike. I hope you can think on your feet here.

While she was spinning around in front of the door in a vain attempt to spot where her family was sitting, the President of the University tapped on the microphone, and then asked everyone to take their seats.

This is it. Here we go.

Jill did not recognize any of the music played as thousands of students streamed in to the floor of the arena, each waving in different directions, bumping into each other, laughing and talking, singing and crying. She numbly followed the person in front of her and found her seat among several hundred arts and science majors, none of whom she knew. She made one more cursory glance around the seats above her as everyone around her stood.

Was that the National Anthem or the School Alma Mater?

She was losing hold of her faculties. She laughed out loud.

"I made a pun! I'm losing my faculties. We're all losing our faculties. We're graduating."

"Shhhhhh! Have a little respect!"

Whirling around, Jill's eyes met those of her old antagonist, Paula. "Hey, I thought you were leaving early."

"I misread the paperwork. I ended up being able to stay." Paula sneered. "What are you doing sitting over here with us anyway?"

"Long story."

"Tell me later." She chimed in on the last line of the Star Spangled Banner.

Jill had never seen Paula like this, and certainly had never heard her sing.

Not a bad voice and she's pretty passionate, too.

When the alma mater was over, everyone in the entire arena sat down in unison. It reminded Jill of the Color War Song Fest competition at camp. After three snaps of the fingers, everyone crossed one leg over the other and sat down in harmony.

"Good morning Ladies and Gentlemen, honored guests, and graduating class of 2017." Jill knew that this was going to be a long drawn out morning. The crawly feelings in her legs and stomach were only just beginning. By now, she was sure; her mother had noticed her name missing under Summa Cum Laude Graduates in Microbiology. Hopefully, she hadn't seen it under Jacobs.

Why this year, of all years, did they include Jacobs' undergrads in this ceremony? Every other damn year they had a separate ceremony.

"It is with great pleasure I present former Secretary Paul O'Neill, who received his Master's Degree in Public Administration here at the University of Indiana."

Snore. I need this to be over.

Jill's stomach was now in full churn.

I wonder if we can get up to use the restroom. Shit, if I do that I am SURE my mother will see me. Oh wait, that's okay. I want her to see me with this bunch of bookworms. "and the world we live in can be a difficult place. It is now up to you, Hoosiers, to make a difference. Good Luck and Go Well. Thank you."
FINALLY. What did he say?

Jill rubbed her eyes and wiggled around in her seat.

When do we throw these things in the air? Or do we?

One by one, the President introduced each little group of majors, with honors students first, and then the whole mass of undergraduates. They all stood up at once, he said pretty much the same things to each college, and they all cheered and tossed their hats in the air.

Jill had cringed when they announced the Summa Cum Laude, the Magna Cum Laude and the Cum Laude when the Jacobs School of Music honored their graduates by name, because she heard her own name echo through the arena. Time stood still. There was, she thought, complete silence. She tried to find her family, or at least Mike, in the stands to see if there had been any kind of reaction, but once again, she couldn't locate them. She inhaled deeply, and then found herself screaming and cheering for all of her friends.

I'll just deal with whatever they know later. For now, it's time to celebrate.

Shit. It's our turn. They're not going to say my name for Summa cum Laude. That's going to be the deal breaker.

And will the College of Arts and Sciences please rise. *...Blah blah blah... is he saying something I should be listening to? It sounds more like the old fax machine signal. God, it hurts my ears.*

Jill reached her hands up and put her hands over her ears. "STOP." She screamed out loud just as everyone around her was screaming and tossing their mortar boards in the air. Tassels were flying loose everywhere and students were jumping up and down.

From behind, two arms clutched Jill around her neck. Paula pulled Jill against the chair and up over the back. Hugging her tightly, Paula yelled into Jill's ear, "Congrats, Roomie. And thanks for putting up with me."

She let go slightly, spinning Jill's small frame around.

"Love you!" She let go.

Off balance, her momentum from the release propelled her forward. She was shocked. "Congrats to you too, I think. And thanks for putting up with me." She was not going to tell this girl she loved her. In fact, she spent four years trying not to tell her how much she hated her. But for some reason, on this day, Jill saw somebody very different in Paula. She saw a confident, accomplished young woman. Not the bitter, angry girl she had moved in with freshman year. "I wish you the best of everything, Paula. Let's be sure to keep in touch." She gathered herself, looking around on the floor for her hat, or at least her tassel.

"I need to go find my "peeps" before this thing is over. Friend me on Facebook or something, okay?"

"Yeah, sure."

Paula sat back down, seemingly disappointed. Jill wondered what she expected of that interchange. Was she suddenly supposed be best friends? Maybe Paula finally realized her error in not being more sociable. Maybe she was scared about changing schools for her Master's degree.

She'll find her way. I have more important things to worry about. Off she went.

Climbing over legs and arms and bodies sprawled out reaching for hats, tassels and hugs, Jill made her way out to the aisle. She attempted to crouch and scoot up the aisle to the back of the set up. All she had to do was make it to the last row and sidle across the back row. The music students were all in the corner back by the micro band. Some of them were even trading off with some of the musicians, as if they were sitting in at an open mike night. Jill giggled to herself.

Won't be long before they're sitting in with my band.
Nestled in and among her people, Jill finally had a settled feeling throughout her body and more importantly, her mind. Everyone was focused on the speaker, the class valedictorian, who just happened to be a Jacobs School of Music graduate of the Historical Performance Institute.

"That guy is amazing."

Jill whispered but nobody was listening to her. She was resigned to paying attention as well, but she couldn't help thinking that she had just risked exposing her deceptive plot for nothing because she had gone totally unnoticed by the people she had snuck over to see.

She jiggled her arm to slide the sleeve of her gown far enough up to see her watch. At least this is almost over.

* * * * *

"I'll have the tuna platter."

Doris closed the menu and looked directly at Jill. "So, was it a typo that your name wasn't in the program?"

This is it… here we go.

"I noticed a beautiful picture of you on the inside back cover, too.

Why didn't you tell us you were in some sort of choir?" Jill froze.

She hadn't seen any pictures. She had glanced through the pictures so quickly, it never dawned on her that there might be photographs from on campus events at which she had been singing. *Shit.*

"Yeah, I called the registrar's office and there wasn't anything they could do about the typo."

Jill was trying hard to use her old "as if" persona. It always seemed to work with her mother. "Oh and I did sing some Christmas carols with the choir a couple years. It was fun." She tried to blow that off. Noticing that Mike was getting ready to say something, she kicked him under the table.

"Ouch."

"What's the matter?"

Doris was always the first one to come to someone's rescue.

"Nothing, I just uncrossed my legs and bumped my knee. I'm fine."

Good boy.

"So, what's your next step, Mike?"

Arnie stretched his arm past Eric's plate to reach for the salt. Doris was sitting quietly to his left, with Ivan to hers. Mike and Jill had just finished ordering, having arrived at the restaurant a few minutes late.

Jill was stalling the inevitable, knowing full well how uncomfortable Mike was in the first place.

"Well, I thought I'd have some lunch, and then maybe go back home for a nap."

Mike was making an attempt at sarcasm, but it didn't sit well with anyone at the table, least of all Arnie Kelly.

"I mean now that Jill is leaving Bloomington. Are you staying here or are you moving on as well?"

"I'm sorry Dr. Kelly, I was just kidding around." Mike changed his tone and got very serious.

"I'm actually headed to New York with Jill, as I've been booked at a few clubs for some steady work just outside the city, and have a few auditions set up for some studio work for a couple of big names."

Mike gulped as all eyes at the table were on him. Jill and he had discussed everything before they left the apartment.

Again, she kicked him under the table.

"Um." Mike picked up his fork and softly drummed it on the table cloth with his left hand.

"I know Jill has a few tough years ahead of her, Dr. Kelly." Jill kicked him again.

"Ow, uh, and I promise you, I will not stand in her way."

"I'm going to hold you to that. Sounds to me as if you're on your way to a career in music. I wish you the best. It's a tough row to hoe."

He stared Mike down. Mike wriggled, revealing his discomfort.

Jill could see that Arnie, too, was dead serious.

She recognized this Dr. Kelly. He wasn't Daddio. He wasn't Dad.

He was Dr. Arnold Kelly, Chief of Cardiology, University of North Carolina Medical Center, Chapel Hill.

"Medicine is a long tradition in this family, Michael. I want to see it stay that way."

Arnie still had the salt shaker in his hand, put it down, and reached for his wine glass. Slouching back into his seat, and revealing a slightly softer side, he continued.

"So, now, let's make a toast to my daughter on her graduation; and to her future medical degree, and to not-so-brutal winters in New York." He held up his glass.

"Oh, and one more thing: to the continued support from her friend Mike."

The Kelly's all raised their glasses, except for Mike. He raised his hand, forming his hand as if he were holding a glass, and in unison they spoke the words, "to Jill."

The guilt was climbing up the inside of her throat. On the one hand she felt terrible about all the lies, but yet she was ready to launch her dreams. And nobody would likely ever make a toast to Jill again.

It will, forever after be, Here's to JayBee.

Chapter 11

They had only been in New York for a year, but it seemed like a lifetime to Jill. Mike had gotten solid work and made a lot of connections but she was struggling. An audition here, a stand-in there, but she wasn't moving along as fast as she had wanted.

My timeline is getting all fucked up. This is not the way it was supposed to happen.

She was bought back to the moment quite suddenly.

"Eighty-six the veal."

The gravelly voice echoed through the hallway of the back kitchen at Chloe's, a mid-priced bar and restaurant on the outskirts of the Upper East Side. Jill looked quickly at her cheat sheet and noticed that she hadn't even written down the veal as one of the specials anyway. She shoved the wrinkled note into the back pocket of her black trousers and slipped her pen behind her ear.

I can't do this anymore.

Just then, her phone began to vibrate in her other back pocket. She dare not answer it. If she got caught one more time she would certainly lose her job.

Why did I tell Dad I got so much in student loans? I had no idea it would cost so much to live up here.

Wondering who would be calling her at work at that hour, she slipped the phone out of her pocket and glanced down to see that it was Arnie. Thankfully, the ringer was off. The last time the phone rang and it sang out that awful rendition of "Heart," she didn't hear the end of the teasing for weeks.

I wonder what he wants. What if something's wrong? He never calls this late. I'll have to call back on break.

Forty-five minutes later, at 11:00 pm, Jill texted her dad to see if it was too late to call. He hadn't left a message so she figured it was either nothing or something too terrible to leave on a phone message. She wasn't going to lose sleep over it. She waited patiently for either a return text or for her phone to vibrate, signaling a return call. Nothing.

Her break came and went with no response, but Jill only had to work until 1:00AM. She went back onto the floor, but there wasn't anyone sitting at any of her tables. She walked over to the bar and leaned up against it, trying to get the attention of the bartender.

David was an amazing mixologist. Not only was he creative in mixing drinks, but he could stun the patrons with fire shows one minute, and entertain them with his guitar or ukulele the next. He was a sweetheart, too. She dare not flirt with him for two reasons. First, she was wearing an engagement ring. Mike had finally proposed after living in New York together for a year. And second, David himself was engaged to a dynamo. In fact, Nancy was her competition. She was extremely talented. She had the voice, but she was also trained in theater and dance… the ultimate triple threat.

"What's eating at you, Jay Bee?"

Jill started using her stage name the minute she stepped out of the car in New York. Nobody north of North Carolina or East of Indiana knows her by Jill Kelly, medical student. Everyone assumes she is a Jacobs trained Opera Singer who is trying to start out a career in rock. David asked again.

"You, okay?"

"Ah, it's nothing. Just I got a call from my father about thirty minutes ago, but he didn't leave a message. When I texted him back, he didn't call or text back."

She sighed. "Not like him, that's all."

David turned away, grabbed a couple of bottles and twirled back around.

"This is going to be good,"

Jill thought to herself. David jumped through all kinds of spins and turns, bottles and glasses flailing and flipping. Pouring into a slender pitcher, he tossed garnishes behind his back, landing them directly in the concoction. Grabbing two brandy glasses by the stems from above his head, he picked up the glass pitcher and delivered it to the other end of the bar. When he returned, Jill asked,

"So, what the hell kind of drink was that?"

"I made that one up. It's called the Fancy Nancy."

He wrinkled up his nose and made a face.

"Nancy suggested that one… it's a really strong drink, and it helps her with cramps."

"Pretty cool the way you do that. So, where's is she tonight?"

"She actually got a small part in an "off off" Broadway show."

"Good for her! What show?"

"I don't even remember the name of it. It's at some obscure theater."

David was multitasking while he was talking. As small as the bar was, he was an icon, and the place was busy. He finally stopped long enough to talk directly to Jill.

"So then, what's the problem?

You don't look happy about the fact that she's in the show." Jill was puzzled at his lack of enthusiasm.

"Just means we have to stay here longer. I really don't like this town."

David had followed Nancy here from Cleveland so that she could take her shot, but he was lonely.

"People here are just not very nice."

"They like you here, that's for sure."

"Yeah, well, I have this crazy neighbor who thinks I'm out to kill her. She's actually called the cops on me twice."

"Really, what happened?"

Jill was running out of break time, but wanted to hear the story.

"I made the mistake of knocking on her door because the mailman delivered some of her mail into my box. She accused me of stealing her mail and whammo, the cops were there in ten minutes."

David's appearance could have been somewhat intimidating to an older woman living alone in New York City. He stood over six feet tall, was very muscular and kept his head shaved. He was covered with ink, displaying some unsavory images, and he wore one of those big rings in one of his ears. Jill never understood those things. She got the tattoos, but the piercing always gave her pause.

"So, what did the cops do?"

"That's the best part."

David began to laugh. His laugh reminded Jill of a cartoon character, but not an evil one. It was certainly incongruous with his appearance.

"The one cop took her into her apartment to talk to her. The other guy told me to forget it... that she had a history of these nuisance calls."

He rolled his eyes.

"That would be fine if that were the end of it, but this morning she lost her shit and started screaming at me in the lobby. 'Monster... Stay away from him; he'll rob you blind...'"

David stopped cold.

His boss had caught his eye, and was shaking his head, so David whispered.

"She's a nutcase. Listen, I gotta get back to work. Talk to you later."

Jill whispered back.

"I think he meant me getting back to work.

See ya!"

Turning on her heels, Jill grabbed her tray and started back toward the kitchen. She noted that she had a couple sitting at one of her tables.

Wonder how long they've been there? Better get over there first.

Abruptly changing her direction, she nearly slammed into another server who was barreling down the aisle.

"Sorry."

"Hi there. Can I get you a drink while you decide?"

"We've been sitting here for ten minutes already. We know what we want." *Bitch.*

"Okay, then, what would you like?"

She had gotten extremely good at pulling off her own ruse, but Jill had never learned how to hide how she felt when people weren't nice.

"Hey, we saw you over at the bar wasting time. Is this your first day on the job or something, or were you just flirting with the bartender?"

The woman was obviously pissed off about other things, Jill thought.

Just breathe deep.

"I do apologize. I'll tell you what. Let me buy you a drink to make up for it. I'll take your food order and put it in, and then buy you a drink on the house while you wait for your food. Would that make it better?"

She had successfully disarmed the customers; however, her boss had overheard the interchange, and while Jill was punching the order into the computer, he came up behind her.

"You can't keep doing that. In fact, this time, the drinks are coming out of your paycheck."

"Yes sir."

This did not even bother jill. She had found that waiting tables was not for her.

She would have to find something else to make some more money until she could get things going, but she knew she couldn't do this anymore.

Again, Jill felt the vibration of her phone. She slipped it out of her pocket. This time, it was a text from her father that read, "Didn't mean to bother U. I thought U might take a break from studying 2 talk. Nothing serious."

Phew. I'll call him in the morning.

* * * * *

"You here?"

Jill slowly opened the door of the tiny one-bedroom apartment. There was so little space, that she and Mike had most of their regular stuff in storage. Mike had been adamant about keeping all of his saxophones with him, even though he only played two of them, so they became the only wall décor they had. Jill had given up her initial idea of getting an upright piano and settled for an electronic keyboard, and they kept only one guitar—an acoustic— not even her electric one.

There was total silence. Mike could easily have been sleeping, but Jill assumed he hadn't gotten home and flipped on the light switch. At almost two in the morning, she was exhausted. Her feet hurt, she smelled like the wine she had spilled down her shirt and she was feeling discouraged. Almost a year had passed, and while she has been able to get away with it all, it didn't look promising to her, this dream she had.

What if I don't make it? What if everything I had planned doesn't happen? I have no degree I can use to go back into science or medicine. I'd have to redo everything. Dad would disown me. What if I've made a horrible mistake?

Jill sat down on the edge of the ratty old futon they were using to double as a couch and accommodations for any sleepover guests. She dropped her shoulders and hung her head, sighing deeply. Within seconds, the tears came. She had been so strong for so long, but she had reached a turning point. She crossed her arms around her back and hugged herself, as a heaviness descended on her.

Suddenly, the creaky door swung open and slammed against the wall. Mike stood in the doorway, arms full, with two saxophones, a backpack, two bags of groceries and a brown paper sack, slightly torn and beginning to fall away from his two-fingered grasp.

"Help me, would ya?" Mike was grinning.

Jill begrudgingly got up from her pity post and drifted over to him.

"Got it," she said, reaching for the torn sack.

"What are you so happy about?"

"Not for me, for you…"

Chapter 12

On the way to the surprise appointment, Mike and Jill stopped by Chloe's to pick up her final check.

She felt a great sense of satisfaction in giving notice. She didn't even feel the need to work for two more weeks because there was a waiting list of servers who wanted to work there. The only thing she regretted was not being able to see David and Nancy every day. They had gotten to be good friends.

What she had, though, was a modicum of success. A light of hope, or at least that was what she was holding onto. It seemed like only a minute ago she was ready to give up.

"I still don't understand how this is supposed to work." Jill had put her complete trust in Mike, leaving her job simply because he said she would be able to concentrate solely on her career from that point on.

Jill slid back into the passenger side of Mike's beat-up Chevy.

Again, she caught her arm on the torn upholstery she pushed down to slide over.

She knew, now, why they didn't manufacture bench seats for smaller cars anymore. Once settled, she continued.

"I mean, am I just giving up the rights to the song altogether so this dame can sing it and make millions, or will I be able to record it myself too, seeing as I wrote it."

"First of all, WE wrote it."

Mike was not about to let her forget that he had a powerful interest in this deal as well.

"We are both on the sales contract, and just so you know, we both retain rights to record it ourselves, either together or individually."

Mike's patience with Jill was growing thin. His career had been moving along enough so that he could make a decent living, and he had already made a lot of good contacts for himself and for Jill as well. Her stubbornness and ego had knocked her out of a few great opportunities.

"Please don't lose your composure this morning. There's a lot at stake here."

"What if I don't like how they are arranging it?"

Jill had crossed her arms over her chest, taking her usual position when she was preparing for a battle.

"Don't I have any say about the integrity of the song?"

"Integrity?" Mike tried not to laugh out loud.

"What?"

Jill knew she should be indignant; just by the way Mike was reacting, but she wasn't quite sure to what he was alluding.

"I don't think you are one to talk about integrity, Jill." Mike had, during their time living together in New York, learned to stand up to Jill when he thought it was challenging his sobriety.

"You've been living a lie for five years. For Christ's sake, Jill, nobody up here even knows your real name besides me."

Jill sat back and looked over her shoulder out the window.

"What if I decide not to sell?"

"Shit. Now you're acting like a child."

Mike's foot rested heavily on the gas pedal.

His slender fingers gripped the steering wheel tightly enough so that, through the corner of her eye, Jill could see his knuckles turning white.

"Okay, okay. I'll listen to what they have to say.

Who is the singer, anyway? Will you at least tell me that?"

"This was supposed to be a fabulous day for you."

Mike was shaking his head back and forth, ever so slightly. He was beginning to show his frustration with Jill after a year of putting opportunities in front of her. This one, she can't blow. "I worked too hard on this one for you to walk in there with this attitude of yours, Jill. I don't care how good you are, and you know I'm you're biggest cheerleader. If I weren't, I would have left you a long time ago."

He stole a quick glance over at her, only to find her still staring out the window, but with her head resting against it.

"I know. I'm sorry."

There was a certain humility that had crept into her voice.

This may just be either my last chance or my big break. I need to stop and breathe.

Jill slowly looked over at Mike, who was again focused on the road. "So, who is it we're meeting?"

Mike took his foot off of the gas pedal, fully expecting some kind of physical reaction.

"Ya ready? I don't think you're going to believe it." He paused, partly because he expected to be punched or hugged, and partly for dramatic effect.

"We are meeting Venus and her people."

"GET OUT OF TOWN!!!" Jill spun around, her left arm swinging, and she proceeded to thrash her arm across Mike's.

"She's as big as they get. How did you do that?"

"Whoa. Slow down." Mike kept his eyes on the road.

"First of all, we are kind of getting out of town. We have to drive out to Long Island where she actually lives.

That's the only way we could work out this meeting, and get to negotiate all parts of the deal."

"What do you mean *ALL* parts?"

"So, here's the biggest part of the surprise."

Mike took a deep breath as the car rolled to a stop at a red light. He slowly turned toward Jill, tilting his head down so he could see her without the distortion of his sunglasses.

"Venus has agreed, as part of the deal, to give you an audition to do two things. One, sing our song as a duet, and two, for a part as a backup singer on her upcoming album and tour."

Jill was speechless. She wasn't feeling what Mike probably thought she was feeling, though. While most people would kill for this opportunity, Jill was actually offended.

"What have you done?"

She shifted in her seat and faced him directly. Whipping off her sunglasses so that he could see her eyes, she began,

"You have no idea who I am, do you? While I thought selling the song would be okay, I am NOBODY'S backup singer. Dammit, Mike."

Now it was Mike who was speechless. The light turned green, saving him from further eye contact. He swallowed hard.

"You're not really mad, are you? You're not really going to turn your back on a leg up into a national tour with one of today's biggest selling pop stars are you? Is your ego that inflated?"

Jill could feel the blood rushing up the back of her neck into her head.

I quit my job for this, to play second fiddle.

"Have you lost total confidence in me? Don't you think I'll make it without riding someone else's coattails? Why do you think I haven't sung with your band? I'm gonna make it on my own. I'm nobody's backup singer."

Mike looked straight ahead. He was biting his lip, using everything he could not to say something he would regret. "Okay," he started, "then we are not going?"

"We can still sell the song, can't we?"

Again, a deep breath. "That wasn't the full deal we had worked out. If we go and change the deal, we may not sell it, and we may not ever get the chance again." The car sputtered to another stop and yet another red light. Mike looked over at Jill, who was in her typical slumped posture, staring out the dirty window.

"Balls in your court.

Do you want me to cancel? I can turn around and go home or we can move forward."

Wiping a tiny tear away, Jill turned back toward Mike. "How did you manage to do this anyway?"

She had been confused as to how this jazz fusion saxophonist who played obscure nightclubs on the outskirts of Manhattan could ever meet and develop business relationships with the pop industry people.

"Who is your contact here?"

"Actually, a few of her band members have become regulars at "7ᵗʰ Avenue" when they're not on tour. They're actually jazz musicians that travel with Venus for a living, but play jazz for life. Kind of like me."

Mike waited for some kind of reaction.

"What do you mean, like you?"

"I didn't know how else to tell you, but I got a job with them." Mike cringed, waiting for the explosion. It didn't come. He continued. "About a month ago, they asked if they could stand in at my club, and we had a blast. We've been playing a lot together, so they invited me to audition. Vee loved the sound, and we've been rehearsing for tour."

"That's why you wanted me to audition for tour?"

It was finally coming together for her. He was taking this job, with or without her.

My career doesn't matter. You were going to go without me. "And the song?

You're pushing me to sell it because you've already been rehearsing it?"

"No, they haven't heard the song. Only Vee heard it. I would never do that to you."

"Really."

"You know Jill, you have gotten so used to lying to everyone else, and you think everyone does."

He knew he had pushed a red button here, but he was tired of abiding by this way of life. "I want you to be there to sing it with her. Wasn't that your dream? What's wrong with a little help?"

The car remained silent for the next few minutes, except for the light rattle emanating from the air-conditioner. Jill stared out the window while Mike kept driving toward their proposed destination. Neither spoke.

* * * * *

With brakes crying, the old Chevy rolled to a stop at one more red light.

The surroundings had changed significantly. What was grey and covered with cement and bill-boards, had become green and filled with sprawling hills and manor houses.

"I'm assuming you're going through with this?"

Mike's first words to Jill sounded sarcastic, yet hopeful. They hadn't spoken for over thirty minutes. The only sounds in the car were the whir of the engine, the rattle of the air-conditioner and an occasional sniff from Jill, who had been weeping to herself.

"I guess so."

"No attitude?"

"No."

"Are you okay with this now?"

"I guess I'll have to be." Jill came across smug, but it was more like surrender.

"Look, Jill, before we get there, you need to know that I did all of this out of love for you and respect for your talent." Mike looked ahead of him on the road to find a place to pull over.

They had already reached a residential area close to their destination, so he pulled up to the curb, put the car in park, and turned to Jill.

"I know you can be the star you've always dreamed of being. But I also know that everyone in this business has to climb a ladder of SOME kind."

He shifted in his seat, pausing as if to recall something buried deep within his soul.

"Look, what you are trying to do is like eating an elephant."

"Huh?"

Jill's puzzled expression spoke volumes. "Now you're talking nuts."

"What I mean is this. Eating an elephant would be a HUGE task… much like building a career. You kind of have to do it one bite at a time. So, how this translates to you is this: What Vee is offering you, is a step stool compared to the ladder she climbed."

"Okay, so it's not peanuts. Ha Ha!"

They both sneered at her feeble attempt at humor. Serious again, Jill continued.

"How does she know I can even sing?"

Mike hung his head and looked down. He wasn't sure how Jill would react to his next admission.

"I took several of your old recordings from college and from when you used to stand in with me at Hoosier Harmony. I even had a copy of your audition tape for Jacobs."

"You didn't."

"Yeah. It turns out Vee has opera training as well. I really think that's why she really wants to meet you."

Jill broke down. Her crying was convulsive, inconsolable. Coughing, gasping and clearing her throat, she tried to speak. Mike leaned in to see whether the tears were angry ones or sad ones, as if he could tell. Having known Jill long enough, he was actually seeing a transformation.

She had been building this artificial life around this imagined career and a phony identity. Only he knew the original Jill… the one who was young, hopeful and innocent.

"Mike, I'm so sorry."

"Don't be. This is how people get started."

He turned off the ignition, reached over and put his arm around his Jay Bee.

"You are going to be something special.

You are special. Nobody is going to care what path you took, except maybe your Dad.

You are going to make it big and your audience is going to love you. I just hope you can hold on to your sense of self through the process."

"Well, I thought I was."

The two sat there in the car, Mike consoling Jill, for a few minutes. Mike tried to slide his arm forward enough to see his watch. They had ten minutes to get there and they were five minutes away.

"You need to pull yourself together and get the snot out of your throat."

"Thanks!"

Jill sat up, reached down to the floor for her purse and rummaged through to find only a ratty napkin she had stuffed in there two weeks ago when they had stopped for subs.

"This will have to do."

She blew her nose, folding the napkin several times.

"La la la la, mi mi mi mi."

"Grammy award winning warm up."

Mike squeezed her one last time, and pulled his arm out to reach for the ignition. He turned the key, but nothing happened.

"SHIT! NOT NOW!" He tried again.

"Don't flood it."

She felt panic rise up inside her. *Great, now that I want this to happen, the fucking car won't start.*

"Hold on."

Mike jumped out of the car having popped the hood.

"I think I know what happened."

Gone for only a minute, he slid back behind the steering, turned the key, and the car turned over immediately.

"Phew. What did you do?"

"I talked to her. And then I said a prayer."

"You have to be kidding me."

"Nope. I believe that if God brings me to it, he'll bring me through it."

Mike had a big grin when he pulled away from the curb.

"Have a sit down."

Chapter 13

She really is larger than life, even in person. I don't think my tongue is working. I guess that's a good thing, because maybe I won't screw this up.

Jill looked around the studio for a place to sit, but there only seemed to be high top stools in front of the mikes. She watched Venus for a cue, but the world class singer stood by the mixing board, back to everyone, sipping on a steaming cup of something.

"Um, should I sit over there?"

"That's fine."

Vee carefully placed her cup down on the mantle of the equipment, and then quickly picked it up again.

"Shit. I'm not in the mood for any surly remarks from Kenny today."

"Who's Kenny?"

Mike hadn't met this one. He only knew some of the instrumental guys.

"He's my self-righteous, pompous, asshole of a sound guy, but he's the best in the business."

She seemed to laugh out loud but was merely clearing her throat.

"He hates it when I put drinks on the equipment."

147

Vee pranced across the thin carpet and situated herself right next to Jill in front a second mike. She held what seemed to Jill to be coffee with one hand, and rested the other on Jill's knee.

"Why you so uptight, honey. This is going to be fun."

"Just in awe of you. You are soooo good."

"I hear you are, too."

For the first time in her life, Jill found herself without words, and had no grace in accepting a compliment. She fumbled around in her head for just the right thing to say. Ultimately, she came up with what she felt to be a profound response.

"Thank you."

"Wanna warm up a little?"

"I guess so."

"No guess so. ALWAYS warm up, whether you're going to sing at the White House or sing Happy Birthday to your three year old niece. ALWAYS be at your best when you sing."

That's my first lesson from the diva. Cut it out. She's not a pretentious, conceited person. She's really approachable. Now behave yourself.

"Okay, lets! Do you just sing a song or two or do you have special vocal exercises that you do?"

"You're going to laugh."

She smacked her hand on Jill's knee and then pulled it away.

"I know that Rod Stewart, no matter what his concert list is, will sing a couple of standards backstage before he goes on. I like to sing a kiddy song or two, and then clear out the pipes with an aria." Vee turned on the stool.

"You have substantial training in opera, right?"

"I do."

"So let's pick something, anything.

We'll start with 'Twinkle, Twinkle, Little Star,' follow up with 'How Much is that Doggie in the Window?', and then bring it home with your choice of an aria."

"I don't know which ones you have the music for."

"Almost all of them. Name your poison."

Mike had found a small chair in the back of the sound booth and parked himself there, saying nothing. He was obviously enjoying the interchange between these two musical artists. He crossed his arms across his chest, grinned and just drank it all in.

"Um, how about Aida?"

"You got it. Let me cue it up to something in Soprano. Hold on. In fact," she added as she hopped off the stool, "I'll cue the system to play all three warm up songs in a row. We'll sing, we'll talk, maybe come to some kind of agreement… and maybe lunch."

Jill was wringing her hands as she watched Vee standing over the soundboard. The star had disappeared when she bent over to fumble around in a drawer. She emerged wearing a pair of thick-lensed glasses in tortoise shell frames. They reminded Jill of her mother's old glasses from when she was growing up.

Must be some kind of retro fashion thing.

"Okay."

Vee climbed back up onto her stool, tapped her mike first, and then reached over to tap Jill's, listening carefully for some evidence that they were live.

"Dammit."

Vee slithered back off her seat and walked over to the sound board. Reaching over the back, she flipped several switches.

"That's better. Now we're cookin' with gas."

She walked back over to the stool and as if almost thinking out loud, she added, "I never did know where that expression came from. My mother used to say it all the time."

I'm the student here. I'm not speaking unless spoken to. Ha ha, that was something my mother used to tell me when she was mad at me.

Jill squirmed around, trying desperately to get comfortable on the stool. It was a little too high, with her short legs, for her feet to rest easily on the cross piece. If they dangled, it would distract her from her singing.

Maybe I should ask if it would be okay if I stood up. No, I don't know what pushes her buttons. I'm NOT saying a word. Bite your tongue, Jill. Bite your tongue.

"Alrighty then." Vee seemed to be happy, now.

"You ready to rock and roll?"

"Yes ma'am."

Whipping her head around, Vee was now indignant.

"Really? Ma'am?"

Jill felt like all of her insides had just collapsed inside. Her throat closed up, her breathing stopped and her heart was now situated in her ears. The pounding was shattering her ability to think.

"Uhh, uhh, I'm sorry."

"Relax, girl, I'm kidding."

Again, Vee put her hand on Jill's knee.

"You are just too uptight. You want something to loosen you up?"

Jill tried to smile.

"No thanks. I'm okay. I am just overwhelmed by the fact that in a minute, I'm going to be singing with you. Just a little nervous, I guess."

"Nervous is good when you're about to go on stage. Keeps you on top of your game." Vee took her glasses off and looked Jill straight in the eye.

"You do not, however, have to be nervous with me. I don't bite. I've been where you are. I also know you have raw talent and are highly trained." She paused. Sound studios are known to be extremely quiet. This one was no different.

You could only hear the sound of their breathing.

"You are going to be something special, and I want to be along for the ride."

Nervous is good. I have to remember that. Did she just say what I thought I heard? Venus thinks I'm going to be something special? SHE wants to be along for the ride?

"Wow!"

Jill tried to make eye contact with Mike, but there was a post obstructing her view. She wasn't even sure if he had heard any of this conversation.

"Thank you. I'm honored."

"Let's make some music." Vee reached down to her belt, and pulled off what Jill originally thought was her phone. It was a remote control for the sound board.

"You ready?"

"I guess it's now or never!"

"You said a mouth full." Again, she giggled.

"My dad used to say that all the time. Never knew where that one came from, either. Okay. I push this button, and we're off." She held up the remote, and then dropped it to her side again.

"I'm not recording this. It's just a warm up." And they sang.

* * * * *

"So, when did you write this song, anyway? Vee put her fork down on her plate, and then picked up her napkin off of her lap to dab the corners of her mouth.

"Some of the lyrical references seem to be a little passé."

"We actually wrote it about three years ago, when we were both living in Bloomington, studying at IU's Jacobs School of Music."

Mike passed on the vegetarian dish that Vee had ordered for lunch and was still waiting for his omelet. He had only some crackers and water. "Jill had come up with the beat in a unique way."

"Tell me."

Jill was still wrapped up in the excitement and having difficulty eating. Every bite was getting stuck in her throat. It was just as well Mike was taking the lead in this part of the conversation.

They had sung together, recording some and playing around some, for almost three hours, so they never did discuss business.

Well," Mike began, "we were just beginning to date.

Jill had been studying for her underclassmen requirements, came up with some kind of beat, and when we were walking across campus on a particularly cold day, she rested her head against my chest, inside my jacket." Mike watched Vee carefully as he spoke, trying not to bore her with too many details.

"The beat of my heart that Jill heard under my jacket reminded her of that same beat she had in her head."

"Well, almost." Jill interrupted.

"It wasn't really until the first time we were intimate that it all came together." She was exhilarated.

"It was the day I got accepted to Jacobs, and I was lying across his chest. Even the chorus,

'I can feel your heart beat' was born that day."

"Oh yeah, that's right."

Mike let her fly, convinced that when it came time to talk contacts, sales, prices, and things like that, Jill was on board. Everything about her demeanor this day seemed to show him that this experience has changed her mind.

"So, you two are a thing?" Vee picked up her tea and sipped carefully through the straw.

Her lipstick, as well as the rest of her make-up, was still in place since early in the morning when they first stepped into the studio. Jill could see why.

"We're engaged, but neither one of us is really sure of what we are engaged in."

Jill flashed a smirk toward Mike, and it was promptly returned. Just then, a white-gloved server appeared from behind the swinging door to the kitchen, and placed a large plate in front of Mike. Just as he had asked, the plate held a feta cheese and tomato omelet, home fries and whole wheat toast, lightly buttered.

"Pretty funny." Vee sat back in her chair.

"Dig in, Mike. When we've finished here, my agent will meet us upstairs in the office and we'll talk turkey." She cocked her head to the side.

"Does anybody know what THAT expression means? Talk turkey?"

"I have no idea. My dad has used that one, too."

Jill put her fork down, and then reached for her napkin. Her entire salad was sitting on top of her lungs. Now, she was beginning to feel the antsy feeling in her legs like she used to feel when she had to do something unpleasant. It wasn't nerves. Vee had made her feel very comfortable. They sounded terrific together, she thought.

Maybe I'm just afraid of what this offer is going to be, or if they're going to offer anything besides buying the song. What if she leaves me hanging out to dry? What if this is all a ruse and she's just using me?

"Any good there, Mike?"

"Delicious! I'm loving it."

"Take your time." Vee looked over at Jill. "So, what is this JayBee stuff about?"

"Just a stage name."

"Bullshit. No, really. You have a name. What is it?"

Jill didn't know whether or not she wanted to go into anything in particular here. This mega-star was asking her some pretty personal questions.

Or is it me? Am I the one that thinks they're too personal? Am I paranoid?

"My given name is Jill Kelly. Kind of boring for the pop world, isn't it?" Jill prayed that her answer would be sufficient.

"True, but there's a reason you selected JayBee." What does it mean?"

Phew. Thought I was going to have to tell her about my dad and the lying. The last thing I want to do is start off on the wrong foot, with Vee thinking

I'm a liar.

"My nickname as a kid was Jelly Bean. Long story. I thought Jelly Bean would be a little silly, so I went with JayBee."

"I like long stories. That way, Mike won't be rushed to eat. Where did Jelly Bean come from?"

Jill took a deep breath and sighed.

"When I was tiny, I couldn't say my whole name, Jill Kelly. Often it sounded more like Jelly." Vee grinned.

Okay, it looks like this might just be enough.

"And since I was a tiny baby, and since I'm not a whole lot bigger these days, my dad used to call me 'Bean,' which kind of morphed into 'Jelly Bean.'" Jill stopped, and reflecting back, remembered how her brothers used to tease her unmercifully, rhyming all kinds of mean and nasty things with her nickname. She sighed again. "Anyway, my dad still calls me Bean. My one brother barely calls me anything. We're not too close at all, but my other brother, Eric, he's the one that actually started calling me JayBee… just short for Jelly Bean. I liked it, it stuck."

"Sounds reasonable." Vee also sighed. "I suppose you have questions about my stage name?"

"I wasn't going to ask."

"It's okay. I don't really share this with anyone on the outside. The paparazzi and the press… they have no idea of who I am and where I came from, and I like it that way."

Vee leaned forward, putting her elbows on the table, crossing her fingers together. Resting her chin on her hands, she began.

"I was one of those kids that everyone picked on. Not just my siblings. I was awkward and clumsy, and I wasn't a very good student."

She turned her wrist and glanced at her watch. "Girls were flat out mean to me."

"Really? You're such a nice person. I don't get it."

"It was, I guess, what you would call bullying today. The only thing I had going for me was my voice. I was a star in the church choir."

"Me too!" *Something else we have in common.*

"I didn't even try to participate in school activities after a while. Not even choir or drama. It was too painful. Hung out with some unsavory characters, got myself in trouble a few times…" Vee stopped cold, second guessing herself. Her eyes darted back and forth for a moment, and then slid her face down into her hands.

"But I'm going to pull the ultimate 'IN YOUR FACE' one of these days."

"What do you mean?"

Confused by this change in her character, Jill tipped her head to the side to see if she could reestablish eye contact. "It sounds like some kind of revenge."

"I think you know I've never appeared in public like you are seeing me today. I'm only wearing my house make-up, right?" Vee picked her head up as if to show off her face.

Hmmm. Sounds a little like what I'm trying to do. For different reasons… "Yes, you usually have some kind of theme to an album or concert tour, with lots of costumes and stuff."

"Well, after this coming tour, I'm planning on doing some television appearances for the first time, and revealing my identity to the public. By the way, my dear, you are sworn to secrecy about all this, got it?" She was dead serious. She turned to Mike, who was sitting there with an empty plate and his mouth wide open, stunned.

"You too, fella."

Oh boy, what have we gotten ourselves into? I hope it's nothing illegal or immoral. She did just say she had gotten herself into some trouble when she was younger. Shit.

"I want all those bitchy girls to see what has happened to me in the ten years since high school. That's all. I've won three Grammies, nominated for four more, I've sold more albums than any other female vocalist before the age of thirty in history, I own four homes on three continents, and I'm President and Founder of three charities... I could go on. Some of them... Well, some of them had to drop out of high school to have babies and raise them alone; some of them are in unhappy marriages because they married for the wrong reasons; there are thousands of reasons why I want to show them why it pays to be kind to people."

Vee suddenly stood up.

"Let's get down to business. Vick is in the office waiting for us."

She started for the door, stopped cold, and turned back to the sound board. "Shit." She went back and flipped all the switches until all of the little red lights went out.

"Okay, now, let's go. Don't forget your stuff."

Mike went to the corner of the sound booth and picked up what he lovingly called his briefcase. It was still his old backpack, but now that there were serious business papers in it, he carried it and himself differently. Jill grabbed her purse, and off they went.

* * * * *

Hesitantly, Vick scribbled out the last line of the third paragraph. His plump belly precluded him from pulling his chair up close to the conference table. He pulled his fountain pen away from the document and slipped the cap on.

"Is that it now? Are we quite finished?"

"I want all parties involved to be comfortable with every phase of this, Vick. I know you thought these kids would be easy, but they're pretty savvy." Vee winked at Jill, who promptly kicked Mike under the table.

"Ouch, what'd you kick me for?"

Leaning in to Jill, Vee laughed,

"They really are all the same, aren't they? They all seem not to know when to shut up."

"Okay, okay, let's get this signed and sealed. I have a 2:00 tee off." Vick was getting impatient. He had already given them a higher percentage on sales of the song, a higher salary for Mike for his tour contract, and for Jill, he just rolled his eyes. The last time he questioned Vee on her decisions, he almost lost his job, so he doesn't reveal any reservations to her about what she wants to do. She's the money maker, after all. "There are four copies that all need original signatures-one for each of us and one for our attorney. Jill, you sign first and then pass to Mike, who will sign underneath."

"You ready?" Mike pulled two ball point pens out of the inside pocket of his jacket and extended one to Jill.

Why are you so calm? Don't you realize what this all means? We are signing away our rights and our freedom to create and to be our own bosses. We're not going to have any authority or decision making power or creative control. I don't think I can do this. God, please tell me what to do. Is this what I wanted? Is this just a stepping stone or will I be stuck in quicksand? What if we come up with a great song? Does she get rights to it because we are under contract? I have so many questions. I'm so scared.

Jill reached for the pen, her hand shaking. Vick had his index finger pressed against the first line on which she had to sign, the tip of which was turning white. Jill noticed the fact that Vick was a nail biter. She placed the pen on the line and scribbled her given name. She looked up at Mike, and silently slid the first document over to him.

It was done.

Chapter 14

"Hi, Dad!"

Jill made every attempt to tone down her voice.

She had almost forgotten what it was like to be a student, but she knew she had to sound tired, overworked, stressed out and having test anxiety, but at the moment she was high; high on the fact that she had a check for $5,000 in her purse. Actually, she had two checks; one for her, and one for Mike.

"Hi Bean! How are you?" Arnie hadn't heard from Jill in a few days.

"I guess you've been overwhelmed with classes, huh?"

"It's a whole new ball game, Dad. A lot more difficult than I'm used to." The words just flowed out of her mouth as if she were actually living that life.

"I'm just glad that the labs are scheduled later in the day."

"I understand. Have you made some new friends this year?

These are the people you're going to go through the tough stuff with. Make sure you have some good study buddies."

Really, dad? Study buddies? I'm not seven anymore. I have to play this through, though.

"Actually, I have. There are two girls that I study with all the time, especially on the weekends when Mike is working."

"Oh, yea, Michael." Arnie always got quiet when Jill mentioned Mike. She sincerely believed he wanted the relationship to break up so she could meet someone with more potential, like someone in the medical field.

"How is he?"

"Oh, Dad, he's doing great. He has two regular gigs, got some really good studio work, and because of that, he's going to be going on tour with, get this, Venus, as the featured saxophonist. There are a couple sets where he's actually going to be highlighted."

"That's nice, Bean. And I've even heard of Venus."

Don't fall all over yourself with excitement. "How's mom? Ivan?"

"They're doing well. Ivan got promoted to Assistant Manager, so that's good." Jill could always sense that tinge of disappointment when she asked Arnie about Ivan. "Mom started volunteering at the nursing home where you used to volunteer."

Jill quietly gasped. *Uh oh.*

"There must be a lot of newer volunteers there. Nobody seems to remember you. Hasn't it only been about five or six years since you were there volunteering?"

Arnie's puzzlement came right through the phone and straight into Jill's stomach, like a flaming arrow.

"They were all pretty old when I was there, Dad. And it has been five or six years." She prayed that would be enough. She tried to change the subject.

"Has Eric heard anything about his internship yet?"

"You would think at least one person would remember you. Not even the volunteer director knows you. I found that kind of strange. Oh well…" Arnie's voice trailed off.

"Dad?"

"Oh, yes, Eric. He hasn't heard anything yet. He was actually trying to get something up in New York, and then come back here for his residency." Arnie's voice took on that familiar parental tone.

"I need somebody up there to keep an eye on you!"

"That would be fun, but then mom would have to send regular care packages."

Jill made every attempt to divert her father from talking about school, medicine and anything else that might get her into trouble. She was just glad Mike wasn't around to hear her end of the conversation.

"Do you not have enough money for food?"

Arnie didn't think she was subsisting well.

She never asked for anything, and he knew what it was costing her to live and go to school in New York.

"I can send you some money, if that's what you need."

"It's not that. Sometimes I just get a little homesick for mom's cooking, for your breakdown of the NCAA, and you know what?

I've been thinking a lot about DeeGee lately." *This would work. He loves talking basketball.*

"Season hasn't started yet. We're still in the beginning of football season. So, are you a Giants fan or a Jets fan?" Arnie asked hopefully, knowing full well that Jill's friend Mike had no interest in sports.

"I don't really have a lot of time to pay attention to football. Most of my non-class time is spent studying or sleeping. Sorry to let ya down Daddio."

"Bean, you haven't called me Daddio in years. Maybe when you come down for Thanksgiving, we can throw caution to the wind and do a little music, that is, if you can still carry a tune."

Jill almost laughed out loud.

Oh, if you only knew.

"I really need to go, Dad. I'm meeting a few friends for dinner and then we're hitting the library." *Lie.*

"Okay Bean, keep in touch when you can, and please don't be afraid to ask for the funds if you need. Eric and Ivan are both officially off the Kelly payroll, so…" Arnie laughed. He was gone.

* * * * *

Jill ran a brush through her hair, staring past her reflection in the mirror.

Do I need to get Vee's approval to cut and dye my hair? I really don't think it's a good idea for me to be so visible without some sort of change to my appearance. It was one thing singing at the Harmony or in choir in college, but this is big.

Putting the brush down, Jill took her hair in both hands and held behind her neck, experimenting with different lengths.

I could do a wild color like orange, or I could do two-toned. I could have it curled in a short perm, or cut it on a strange angle. Naw, none of that is me.

What should I do? Maybe just orange and a short bob cut.

Remembering that she had picked up a few magazines at the corner drug store, she plopped down on the couch and started thumbing through them looking for ideas for her new image.

Vee does it with make-up and costumes, but I'll have to wear what she tells me to. I only have control over my hair. Maybe I can call her to discuss it? No, I don't have the right to do that. I'm only under contract for one day, and we haven't even had the first rehearsal yet.

She continued to flip through the pages, occasionally reading a short article or two. For some reason she had no power to concentrate.

Where the hell is Mike? It's almost three in the morning. He should have been home an hour ago. Maybe they had him play another set. No, they close at one on Sundays. Why am I talking to myself? I don't even have anyone to call because he left his fucking cell phone here.

Shit where is he? He probably thinks I already went to sleep so he's not rushing. You know what? I'm going to sleep. Or at least I'm going to try. I'll go to the bank in the morning. I didn't want to make that big a deposit in the ATM. What was I doing? Oh yeah, going to bed.

Jill pressed through her evening ablutions and climbed into bed. Exhausted, more from her mental activity than anything else, she fell into bed, but could not fall off to sleep quickly. She finally got up and popped a Xanax. Back in bed, but one to dream vividly, she fell into a sound sleep despite the fact that she had left the lights and the television on in the tiny apartment.

* * * * *

"She said they would forward a rehearsal, recording and travel schedule next week. Does that mean I don't have anything at all to do until then?" Jill was in unfamiliar territory. She had always had a schedule whether it was for school or work, extra-curricular activities or choir, church or chores. She looked at Mike quizzically as he played around trying desperately to tie his tie.

"And why do you have to go to the studio for rehearsal and I don't? And can I be there even if I'm not scheduled?"

"Calm down." Mike turned to Jill, still trying to straighten his tie. It was the same tie he wore Saturday to Jill's audition, and the stain from his lunch was still evident. "This rehearsal is for the band only. Vee won't even be there. I think she's out in California doing some talk show."

"So what should I do?"

"I have a couple of ideas. First, go to the bank and deposit the money!" Mike twisted back for one more look.

"Still not straight. Oh, and if you could, please buy a couple of ties for me. I don't know why, but we have to wear ties to rehearsal."

"I get to go shopping? Woo Hoo!"

Jill didn't remember the last time she bought something new. She had been doing all of her shopping at the second hand shops as her budget allowed for nothing in the way of wardrobe. As long as she had the black jeans for her serving job, and an outfit or two for auditions, she had been fine.

"Why don't you see about a slightly bigger apartment, too? I mean, if we just went under contract and we're guaranteed ten grand a month for the six months, not including whatever royalties from the song, I think we can afford to live a little further out in a bigger place, don't you?"

The thought of a bigger apartment knocked Jill back, enough to sit her down on the old couch. It hadn't dawned on her this money, the checks she was now holding in her hand, were going to come *every* month. Lost in thought, she didn't answer.

"Hello? Jill?"

"Maybe a two bedroom with one as a music room or studio?" She was imagining a place to write more music, collaborate on songs with Mike, play, record and mix JayBee's first album…

"Jill?" Mike knew she was off somewhere else.

"I don't think an apartment building would tolerate a music studio. Neighbors don't usually appreciate that kind of noise."

"But we'll be stars… they'll let us. We can sound proof it."

"Yo, elephant girl… one bite at a time, remember?"

"Oh shut up and go to work." Jill got up, grabbed her purse and keys and left him standing there in the middle of the conversation. Something stopped her before she slammed the door. She poked her head back in and added one more snide remark.

"Your tie is still crooked."

"Thanks loads." Mike finished primping and then ordered a car to pick him up to take him out to the studio.

* * * * *

I hate driving this wreck. We need to get a car. That's what we need to get with some of this money.

The car had started shaking while she was in line at the drive through window at the bank, an omen of things to come. Jill lurched and staggered up the last hill to the mall nearest their apartment, hoping the car would make it. She turned right, into the driveway of the parking lot, just as the old Chevy gave out.

Able to coast on the last of the acceleration, Jill manipulated the car into the nearest parking space and shifted it into park. She grabbed the parking brake lever as if she were still angry at Mike and yanked it as hard as she could, knowing that if she didn't it wouldn't stick.

Reaching over for her purse, Jill realized she would have to deal with the dead car at some point, but decided to go shopping first. She jumped out of the car and slammed the door shut. For a split second, she thought the door was going to fall off.

Oh, come on, it's not that bad. You're just angry. Now go in and buy him the ugliest ties you can find. Boy, when I get angry, I stay angry. I'm going to go in there and buy myself something to make me feel better.

"Thank you." Jill turned back to speak to the man that had held the door open for her, but he was gone.

So much for the kindness of strangers! Oh man, that would make a great premise for a song. Especially in this crazy world we live in. A guy does something nice for you and when you try to say thank you, he walks away. Now how can I translate that into lyrics? Why am I talking to myself again? There are plenty of people around. Did I say that out loud?

"Excuse me, but could you tell me where I might find a men's store in this mall?" She stopped at the nearest information kiosk.

"You just walked past one. Turn around, lady. It's right there." The young man in the kiosk was looking at Jill like she was from outer space.

"Sorry, I was otherwise engaged."

Why did I say that? I'm not the pretentious type. I was lost in my head. Kind of like I am now. I must be losing my mind. Here I go again. At least I'm not hearing voices. I heard that people that are really mentally ill hear voices. Hello? Well, nobody answered.

Stop it, Jill. Go in a store and talk to a person. Geez. What is wrong with me?

Jill turned around and spotted the men's store and walked over. None of the mannequins in the window looked anything like Mike. They are all dressed in business clothes. Mike's wardrobe is mostly jeans with striped or small patterned shirts, usually cotton. Jill decided to go in and see what they had.

"Good morning," came a voice from behind her.

"Oh, hello. You startled me. I was looking for some ties."

"Why, it's nowhere near Father's Day." He chuckled, as if his joking were worldly and sophisticated.

"My fiancé needs two or three solid color ties, with or without patterns." Jill gave no credence to the attempt at humor. She was focused on the task at hand, and maintaining her own composure.

The salesman cleared his throat. "Follow me."

The solid color ties were neatly laid out in cascades on a long table in the back of the store. The printed ones hung on tiered racks behind the table. Jill thanked the salesman and began looking.

"Uh, please let me know if I can help you with anything else. If and when you've selected something, I'll be happy to ring that up for you."

Must be on commission. Like working for tips. I get it.

"Okay, thank you."

Jill thumbed through shades of grey, blue, pink and green but found herself to be totally indecisive. She had started out the morning full of anger, yet now she was fighting panic. She looked up but did not immediately see her salesman.

Her eyes darted around the store. *Must be on a break. I need to be able to complete this simple task or I'm driving myself to the emergency room.*

Jill's heart was thumping in her chest. *This was not the Bum bum Bum bum of a song. This was a heart attack coming on. I'm gonna die. What's wrong with me? Does he even have a gray shirt? He can wear this one with anything.*

Jill looked for the salesman again. *Oh good, there he is. Maybe I can get a drink of water and sit down for a minute. I like the green one; not that one, it's too green. Is he heading over here? No, he said I should ask him if I need anything. I need him to call 9-1-1. No, I don't I'll be okay. Just breathe, dammit.*

Jill put the three ties that she had selected down, on top of the display, and walked gingerly over to the service area. The salesman was standing there, behind the cash register.

"I don't suppose you have any cold water?" Jill was shaking noticeably.

"Ma'am, are you okay? Do you need medical attention?" The salesman seemed alarmed. Jill face had grown ashen, her lips white.

"I don't think so. If I could just get some cold water to sip on, I think I'll be just fine." As the last words slipped out, Jill could feel her legs giving out from under her.

* * * * *

"Too many bites of elephant today."

"Huh?" The salesman had rolled up some tee-shirts and slipped under Jill's head after calling emergency. The mall security responded immediately, however she was breathing and her heart rate was strong, although a little fast. "Lady, you passed out."

"I'm sorry. I don't know what happened." Jill tried to sit up, but the security guard and the salesman, on either side of her, held her shoulders and kept her down.

"We can give you some cool water to drink, but you aren't going anywhere until the EMT guys say you are. And that will be any minute." The salesman looked concerned, although Jill's color had returned to normal and her lips were pink again. "Did you want those three ties?"

"Ain't that just like you guys? You'll do anything for a commission." The security guard snapped at the salesman, and Jill could plainly see there was no love lost between them.

"Actually, I do. If you'll hand me my purse, I can give you the credit card." Jill wanted to be sure she accomplished at least one of the things Mike asked her to do.

So, I won't go apartment shopping. He'll have to do that with me.

The salesman sneered at the security guard while he rung up the sale.

"Will you be needing a gift box?"

"No thank you. I really think I can sit up now." Jill managed to get up to her elbows, high enough to spot the back of one the EMT guys walking backwards, weaving his way through the clothing racks to the back of the store.

* * * * *

Anxiety attack. Hmmm! Me? I didn't think I was the type. What is the type anyway? Oh shit. Now I have to deal with his fucking car.

Jill walked out of the mall carrying her purse, the bag of ties and the obligatory box from the chocolate shop. Through all of the excitement, she did not forget that her intention was to buy herself a treat. She reached the car and popped open the trunk, depositing the two bags gently in amongst the various musical instruments, boxes and auto paraphernalia.

Making every attempt to remain calm, partly because of what the medical people said and partly because of her history with the car, she climbed in and slipped the key into the ignition. Jill put on the seat belt, and then rummaged through her purse, looking for the hidden pack of cigarettes. She stopped. "Mike will smell it immediately if I smoke in the car." Instead, she reached again for the key, took a deep breath and turned the car on. Save a few sputters, the old Chevy came through. Jill shifted the car into reverse, backed out and drove home.

* * * * *

Okay, we made it home. I did the bank and the ties. I'm just gonna go upstairs, have some lunch and take a nap. I just need to calm down and figure out what's going on with me. I could talk to

Eric about all this. He would know. Things are getting a little too crazy.

I'm starting to get really uncomfortable lying to Dad. Starting to? Maybe Mike was right.

Maybe I'm not the same person he met that day at registration. Maybe I have lost myself in all the lies. Nah. I have this whole thing figured out. No, I don't. My Daddio has always trusted me. He still thinks I'm going to be a doctor. He's going to hate me for lying. But I'm going to be a big star. I've already made it past all those horrible statistics he warned me about. But I've been lying to him. I've been taking his money for a big fat lie. Too bad. I can't stop now. He'll know soon enough and I can pay him back. The money, at least...

Chapter 15

"Hey Mike, is this normal? I mean, do all traveling bands and singers do this?" Jill was in awe of her surroundings.

She never expected first class hotel accommodations. Granted, they had a small room and Vee was up in the penthouse suite, but still…

"I somehow had this idea we'd be remanded to some fleabag motel close to the arena and left on our own. According to this, we have to be upstairs in Vee's suite at 4:00, but until then we can do what we want."

Jill was sitting on the edge of the bed perusing the travel agenda for her first road trip.

"I'm a little surprised myself." Mike was hanging up his jacket in the closet. "I want to see if I can find a meeting nearby. Feeling like I really need to check in."

"You okay?"

"Yeah, I guess."

"No, you're not." Jill knew Mike. He always qualified things with 'I guess' when he was teetering, and didn't really know how he felt.

"I'm a little nervous about tonight, that's all."

"Me too! But this is it. This is our chance."

"Jill, there is something bothering me." Mike sat down next to her on the edge of the bed.

"You do realize that what is happening to you is very unusual, right?"

"Well, I guess so. I've worked hard to get here."

"Have you?" Mike waited for the explosion.

"Of course, I have, why, you don't think I have?

"I'm not looking for a pat on the back. You know I don't have an ego, but you have to be honest with yourself. You've been living in the shadow of all of this double life, that I' think you haven't really noticed the true path that got you here." Mike took a deep breath. Jill just stared at him.

"Even Vee knows you have something underneath that you are hiding."

"She does? What did she say? Did she ask you something? Did you tell her anything?" Alarmed by the possibility of betrayal, she jumped to her feet.

"What, Mike, what?

"I didn't tell her anything. She's just very intuitive. Remember that she has a past of her own that she is just now revealing…" Mike tried to parallel Vee to Jill's story but they were nothing alike.

"The difference is that she was running away from something bad to something good. You are running away from something good, that if you continue without being honest with your family and more importantly yourself, you're going to have problems." Mike's eyes met hers.

"I love you baby, but this is all beginning to burn a hole in me."

"Hey, that's on you. I told you, as soon as I make it big on my own, I will tell them all."

Jill was ready to throw another tantrum and leave, but thought better of it since they were in a plush hotel in a strange city. If anyone were going to leave it would be him. "Go, go find your meeting. Sounds like you need one."

"Not nice." Mike stood up.

"Think about this while I'm gone. You never would have met Vee if it hadn't been for me. You would still be waiting tables while I was the one paying the dues to make it in music. Just remember that." He grabbed his jacket and phone and he was gone.

"Fine!" Jill didn't speak loud enough for him to hear it, because she didn't want him to come back. The last time she did that, the fight erupted into viciousness and she was already uneasy enough about the concert looming that night. She found her purse sitting on the armchair and rifled through it to find the small bottle of pills she had hidden in the bottom.

If Mike knew I was doing this it would be the end of us for sure. They said it would take away the anxiety. I better do it now because I don't want to be sleepy later.

* * * * *

"Hey, you, I'm sorry." Mike gently shook Jill.

"Wake up. I didn't mean to dump on you, especially today." He shook her more, and finally was able to rouse her from the deep sleep.

"Did you at least eat something? I brought up a small salad from the café downstairs just in case."

Jill rolled over on her purse. *Thank God I put that bottle away. Or did I? How many did I take? Doesn't matter now. I'm awake.* "Oh, hi. How long were you gone? What time is it?"

"It's almost three thirty. You need to eat and shower and get dressed. We have to be upstairs soon."

"Did you find a meeting?"

"Yeah. There's a church a few blocks away that had one at noon." Mike sat on the edge of the bed.

"Honey, I'm sorry. I felt like I needed to say SOMETHING, but I guess my own emotions got in the way and I didn't say it right or I didn't say it nicely." He started to weep.

"You know I believe in you. You KNOW I think you have what it takes to be the star you want to be." He sniffed and then wiped back a tear.

"I just don't want you to lose the love and respect of your family at home while on this journey of yours." Mike, contemplative, continued.

"You know that I lost my whole family because of my manipulative behavior… It has taken me years to make my way ever so slowly back into their lives. They have had such a hard time learning to trust me again."

Jill sat up, silently.

"The most important thing I've learned in working the program and staying clean and sober is to live an honest life. You know that, right?"

Jill nodded her head, still hushed.

"So, you understand why it makes me so uncomfortable perpetuating your double life right along with you." Mike tilted his head down, and with puppy dog eyes, begged for approval.

Again, a silent nod.

"Can we put this afternoon behind us and play and sing like we never have before tonight?" Mike's voice started to climb in energy and volume.

"Can we support Vee and make her confident that she picked the right team for her tour?"

Reaching a crescendo, he finished with "Let's go sing "I Can Hear Your Heart Beat!" and drive it up the charts to NUMBER ONE!"

"Oh Yeah!" Jill jumped up off the bed.

"Let's do it!" She grabbed the salad from him, sat down at the small table and wolfed it down. Within minutes, she was in the shower doing vocal exercises, and practicing her parts for the show.

"Hey Mike…"

Mike poked his head through the crack in the open door of the bathroom.

"I just had a great idea for another song."

"That's my girl!"

*****

The hotel van barely had enough room for the band, much less the extra instruments some of them had brought with them. Vee was taking her limo along with her agent and a few friends, but all of the newbies had to find their way to the venue themselves. Jill and Mike almost felt better that this was the protocol. The drummer was with Vee. He had been since they were in college, so nobody said a word.

"Hey man, can you just send another van around. We can't do this with just the one."

"No problem, sir."

The valet picked up the phone and within three minutes, another van pulled around from the back. Jill stayed with the singers and two of the musicians. Mike joined the horn section and all of the extra equipment on the other van.

"What time was load in anyway?" Mike asked one of the other guys on the bus.

He knew some of the terminology, but had never done a gig at such a huge venue before.

"We have to be in and set up by six. The gates open at seven and we aren't to be anywhere in view." Mo played the clarinet with the band. He had been with Vee on her last tour, so he knew the procedure.

"In fact, Vee has ordered dinner for everyone backstage, to be delivered right at six. We can hang out there or go out for dinner, but we would have to be in by seven through the back door. She is adamant about it."

"Hey, I'm not messing with rules… not on my first gig on my first tour with the likes of Venus." Mike sat back in the seat, both of his saxophone nestled between in legs in soft cases. He usually traveled with hard cases except on the night of a concert because he never put the instruments down or out of his sight on those nights. Almost like a newborn baby, he cradled them, as they were his own children.

The two vans pulled around to what would serve as the stage door of the United Center. Vee's limo was already parked and empty. The musicians carefully unloaded their instruments and additional equipment and entered through the back door.

Mike and Jill walked slowly, drinking in the magnitude of the building. The last time Jill could recall being in a building that big was when she graduated from college, and before that, it was to go see a Hornets game with her dad in Charlotte.

Oh Daddio, if only you could see me now.

Vee was already on stage dancing around doing sound checks from every possible corner that didn't have a speaker or a sound mixer already set up. "Wait, wait, wait… hold it." She was waving her arms.

"There's something wrong with the balance and I don't like how the floor feels over here. Can we get someone to rough it up a little or I'll end up on my ass." She flitted over to the sound guy that was sitting at the moveable unit and handed him a mike.

"Let me have the boutonniere mike now. Is it ready?"

She clipped it to her collar and tried the whole thing again. She repeated the process with a headset mike, and then returning the equipment turned to the rest of the band setting up and snipped,

"I'm done, call me when you're ready to do the full check. I'm in the back."

Jill stood frozen, watching every move Vee made. *That's going to be me, very soon. I'm going to be the one getting first dibs at the sound guy, telling everyone what to do, and then relaxing until show time. After all, they will be coming to see me, JAYBEE.*

When all was set up, Mo was the one elected to go back to her dressing room and retrieve Venus. She was already half dressed in the costume for the opening number, and it was fifteen minutes before six. "Right on schedule," she said as she bounced out onto the stage.

You guys are the greatest! Okay, one quick number, because I know you got it right the first time." She took the headset, slipped it on and stood right in the middle of her pack of backup singers, including Jill.

"Wait, did somebody fix the floor?" That was one thing Vee couldn't rely on her own staff to repair. The United Center was not her favorite venue, and she had some trouble last time.

"JayBee, go check over there that nobody will slip during the dance set."

Jill walked over and gingerly ran her foot over and around the area Vee had indicated. "It seems fine to me."

"Okay then, let's get this show on the road. Oh holy… there's another one of those expressions. We're already on the road." Vee loved to laugh at her own silly jokes.

"Okay, hit it Kenny."

* * * * *

"Backstage at the United Center is a whole different world than was at the Harmony Club in Bloomington, Indiana. It isn't dark and dingy. It certainly isn't small. There's a whole underground network of offices and conference rooms that probably nobody on the outside even knows about." Jill spoke to Mike as if he wasn't standing next to her and wasn't able to see for himself. She was stunned by the enormity.

"So where is Vee's dressing room?"

"I think we're supposed to meet in one of those conference rooms for the dinner."

Jill took Mike by the hand and led him. He had both of his saxophones slung over his shoulder.

He refused to leave either on stage like the rest of the musicians. Jill was almost running, like a child let loose at an amusement park.

"Come on…"

The door to the conference room to which they were headed was slightly ajar. Vee sat quietly in the corner, sipping a cup of tea. The table was covered from one end to the other, with all kinds of healthy foods. Mike glanced from one end to the other, squinting with displeasure.

He leaned over to Jill and whispered, "Not one piece of meat. No chicken. Not even fish. It's all that health food Keenwah stuff."

Jill whispered back. "Suck it up just this once. Besides, the quinoa is pretty good. It looks like there are some pungent vegetables mixed in, so you will at least have some flavor this time."

Mike whispered again. "Do you mind if I go grab a hamburger?

"Yes!"

"Hi there!" Jill made every attempt to ignore Mike's last question and enter the room on an upbeat note. Vee, however, seemed to be in some kind of trance.

She didn't look up. She didn't respond. Jill tried again. "Hi Vee, we came in to grab a bite."

"Oh yeah, hi. Help yourself." Vee returned to her meditative state.

Mike whispered, "Oh I heard about this. She won't talk to anyone now until show time. She gets into this dazed kind of trance pre-show. It's kind of like a pre-performance ritual."

"Oh, okay, well then let's eat and go." Jill picked up a plate, filled it with salads and fruits, and grabbed some French bread and a bottle of mineral water. Mike stuck to cheese and bread and put an apple in his pocket. He looked for a soda, but there was nothing but weird juices and water. He took a bottle of vitamin water, turned and took one last glance at Vee and headed for the door. "Aren't we supposed to eat here?"

"No. Let's take it back to our green room."

Mike was very uncomfortable in the conference room. Once they were back in the hall, he asked, "Don't you find her a little bizarre?"

"Nah, she is just a health food aficionado with a pre-game ritual. A lot of athletes do stuff like that."

"I wouldn't know."

Mike led the way down the hall back to the green room. Just off to the right were the two designated dressing rooms. The athletes who played in the arena had locker rooms in a separate area, with full showers and baths, exercise rooms, training facilities and classrooms. "This place is massive," said Jill.

After eating, they parted ways into their respective dressing rooms, to get ready for their debut as performers on a world class tour. Neither one had any idea what tomorrow would bring. They were both, finally, focused just on the moment. This was the way

Mike lived his life every day. This was how Jill was portraying the neophyte.

Maybe he did make the inroads for me. Maybe I do owe a debt of gratitude to him. It probably never would have happened this quickly. Maybe I'm not as good as I thought I was. I never played to an audience this big. What if I freeze up? What if I forget the dance moves? Or worse, the words? Oh god, what have I gotten myself into. This is no fucking neighborhood bar, Jill. This isn't your Sunday church choir. Oh God. I can't do it.

Jill looked back over her shoulder to see that Mike had disappeared into the Men's Dressing room. She took a deep breath and held it, turned on her heels, and started down the hall in the opposite direction. The further she got from the green room the faster her heart was beating. Bum bum Bum bum Bum bum.

Jill stopped suddenly. She felt the beat in her ears. Bum bum Bum bum Bum bum. She collapsed into a heap on the floor, hyperventilating. She leaned against the wall, and within a minute, she was out cold.

I need to run. I can't stand it anymore. I don't know where I'm running, but I have to get away from this feeling.

"Hey, JayBee, man, what's doing, you okay?" This time it was Kenny who found her. "Are you doing downers or are you sick?" He gently tried to rouse her. "Did you fall?"

"Nah. No. I'm okay." Jill roused herself as quickly as possible. "I just got a little lightheaded, so I got down on the floor in case something happened. Really, I'm okay."

"Do I need to call 9-1-1?" Kenny had a soft side.

His next question was the one Jill was afraid of. "Do you need me to tell Vee you can't go on?"

"Oh, heavens, no." Jill sat up straight. "After all of the rehearsals, I'm not missing this for anything." Jill surprised even herself this time. She was just about out the back door, ready to bolt on the performance, and here she was lying about how ready she was to go on.

"I'll get you some water. Do you think you can make it down to the green room?" Kenny helped her up to her feet.

"Sure, Ken. Really, I'm fine."

"Want me to go get Mike."

"Absolutely do not. Why upset him?"

If he knew I was either running or panicking, it would only prove he has been right all along. I can't ever let him know that.

Jill started back down the hall. In fact, I'm a little short on time, so I'll just go get ready. There's cold water in the dressing room. Thanks, Kenny"

"Okay. I was just going to come down there and let everyone know that Vee said to meet in the conference room in about fifteen minutes. Can you make that announcement to the girls in the dressing room for me?"

"Sure, Kenny."

* * * * *

"Ladies and Gentlemen, put your hands together and make some noise for Venus…"

Everything in the building was pitch black, save a trail of tea lights that marked a hidden path for the musicians to find their way onto the stage. Vee was up on a platform above the drummer, ready for her entrance. The back-up singers were lined up offstage, half on each side. A single spotlight started to glow ever so slightly over her head as Vee lifted the handheld microphone to her chin. Her voice started out low and as it grew, the light got brighter and crowd screamed louder. Jill was mesmerized by the entire process.

By the time her first song was over, Vee owned the arena.

Whatever made me think I could ever perform that way? I'm just happy to be a part of the show to witness her expertise.

The music shifted, the lights came up at the foot of the stage and the six back up dancers/singers threaded their way in a serpentine onto the stage and launched into an upbeat refrain. Spinning and singing, Vee joined them down on the floor and then danced out in front of them to burst into the first verse of Jill's song.

There it is… the debut of my first rock song. Do they like it? They seem to be moving and dancing in the seats. Ooh my turn to sing.

"I can feel you're your heart beat…"

* * * * *

"What a rush!" Jill was flying down the hall to the dressing room.

"What a fucking rush! Did you hear those people? Wasn't that just astounding?"

"Wait for me!" Mike could hardly keep up with her.

"Slow down, you." Mike had to break into a trot to catch up with Jill.

"She's amazing, isn't she?"

"Thanks Mike, thank you so much for introducing me to her… for helping me get this leg up. You were right. I didn't earn this opportunity, but I sure do appreciate it. I appreciate you. I love you. I love Vee. I love life!"

"Whoa, are you high?"

"I'm high from being out there."

Besides, I was taking benzos… they don't bring you up, they calm you down. I'm okay. I'll stop using them now that I've gotten past this first show.

"I'm just so happy, that's all. Next stop, Milwaukee."

Chapter 16

"Hello gators!" Vee wasn't set up to do the show at the University of Florida in Gainesville the same way she had in all of the other shows so far, so the rehearsal and meeting had a change in the song set.

This was the first outside stadium, and the biggest audience so far. The concert opened with everyone on stage and Vee walked on when she was introduced.

The crowd was wild. The smell of beer was strong in the air. Swirls of smoke danced in front of the footlights.

"Let's do some music."

Vee turned around, raised her right hand and then slashed it down, signaling the powerful slam into "Great Shakes," the number one song from her last album. A raucous, rowdy song, it got the entire stadium quivering with electricity. When the song was over, Vee looked straight at Jill, and with one finger, motioned her to come towards her. Jill felt a chill attack her. She cocked her head to the side as if to question.

Vee slowly nodded.

"Cool it kids. I have some business to take care of here." The audience paid no attention.

They continued to cheer and clap. "This One's On You," they yelled.

"Eat My Dust." Yelling and screaming some of her hits, the masses weren't interested in talk.

They clearly wanted music. As Jill approached Vee, the drummer kicked in with a loud drum roll and kicked it with a loud hammer to the crash cymbals.

"Hey peeps, I want you to meet somebody tonight. This is my friend JayBee. Now be nice and say hi JayBee."

I don't believe this. What is she doing to me? Wait! They're actually listening to her. They're saying hi JayBee.

"I happened upon this young lady in New York a few months ago. She's agreed, whether she knows it or not, to sing a duet with me. So, here's JayBee and me, and the song is, 'I Can Feel Your Heart Beat." The music started. Jill could barely hear it. She couldn't feel the mike in her hand.

She stood there, her insides shaking, next to the biggest rock star in the world, and she was supposed to sing a duet.

What part should I sing? Are we doing harmony? Do I go first or will you? Are you trying to ruin my career? What the fuck? Oh God.

"I can hear your heart beat… I can feel your heart feel, I can know your thoughts as if we were one…" sang Jill. The stadium became quiet. Vee kicked in with the next line, so Jill stopped singing. When she reached the chorus, she motioned Jill to join her. They sang together. The more comfortable Jill got, the more Vee backed away. Before the next chorus, Jill 'owned' the audience as Vee had. She launched into the chorus alone, and Vee disappeared to the back of the stage and leaned on Mo's shoulder. Mo looked right at her and winked.

As the last refrain approached, Jill was on different spiritual plain. She hadn't even noticed that Vee wasn't singing with her, that the crowd was moving to her rhythm and that it was Mike alone who was accompanying her, with just a little help from the drummer.

The audience exploded into applause and whistles. There was no hooting or booing. There were no hooks to drag her off the stage.

She graciously bowed, and then turned to find her mentor. Vee had started walking toward her, clapping her hands above her head. They embraced. Vee whispered into Jill's ear.

"Don't get used to it… this is still my show, kitty." Then she gave her a big wet kiss on the cheek and smacked her on the rear. "Now get back to the line."

The rest of the show in Gainesville was a blur. Jill seemed to go through the motions but had no idea what she sang or danced. It was all secondary to that moment. That moment that Vee had just given her.

* * * * *

"So, did you know she was going to do that?" Jill was struggling with the knot in the shoelaces on her sneakers.

"You must have known something because you were playing alone with me."

"Funny, I didn't think you even noticed." Mike stood in the doorway of the dressing room. Accommodations at Ben Hill Griffin Stadium were not as plush as some of the professional sports arenas that had been playing.

"But yes, I knew."

"Why didn't you tell me? You know I could have freaked out and messed up the whole thing."

"Why would I ever even think that? This is what you've always dreamed of for as long as I've known you." Mike crossed his arms and settled in against the door jamb. "I've never seen you even miss a beat in any performance. You seem to float when you're on stage."

"Okay. Fine." Jill was frustrated with the sneaker and tossed it at Mike.

"Fix this, will you, please?"

"Are you mad at me?"

"No." *But I need to tell you something.*

"It seems like you are." Mike bent over and picked up the sneaker. His patience with things like this was much better than Jill's was with anything.

"Just know that Vee told me not to tell you, and she's the boss, okay?"

"Yeah, I guess. But you know you're my fiancé. Keeping something like that from me is pretty big, dontcha think?"

I get it. Oh God Mike, I need to tell you that you were completely right. I'm losing my mind. I'm relying on the Xanax too much. I have to come clean.

"I imagine I could have told her that. I just thought her surprise would mean so much more this way. She thinks you're ready. I have other things she's planned… but let me ask her before I tell you anymore." He got the lace untied and tossed it back.

"Okay?"

"I can't take any more surprises. What could she possibly do that was better for my career than what she did tonight?"

"Let me talk to her first." Mike wasn't budging. "Come on. Let's get back to the hotel and get something to eat.

The two walked hand in hand out of the stadium onto the campus of the University of Florida.

It was January, but the temperature was only in the low 50's. This was unusual for both of them, having spent the last six years in Bloomington and New York. Jill rested her head on Mike's chest once again, looking for that familiar sound that soothed her soul. They walked slowly across the street toward the parking lot by the basketball arena. There was still electricity in the air from the concert, and plenty of students milling around the corner of Stadium Road.

"Hey, isn't that the one who sang solo tonight?" came a voice from behind them.

"Yeah, what'd Vee say her name was? Jay something? Cee – no JayBee. Come on."

Jill picked her head up and looked back over her shoulder to find two young girls running up behind them.

"Hey, can we get your autograph?"

"Me, really?"

Mike stepped away. "Nobody ever wants the sax player's autograph… of course, you."

* * * * *

There were only three more stops before the Venus tour promoting her new album would be finishing up in New York, but Jill and Mike were both exhausted. They parked the rental car in a spot close to the entrance of the hotel, and leaving all of the equipment locked in the trunk, staggered into the lobby and headed straight for the elevator. The rest of the band was out on University Drive drinking in the college ambiance, and hanging out with the students. Mike was pretty sure they were getting high as well. He had stopped doing that after the first stop on the tour in Chicago, since the temptation was too great.

The hotel room was warm as they had left the heat running.

"January in just a sweater! Who knew?" Jill crossed her arms and wiggled out of her cashmere and tossed it on the bed.

"I'm gonna hop in the shower. Do you wanna order something from downstairs to eat or just munch out on the junk in the honor bar? I'm in the shower."

She barely heard him as she closed the bathroom door.

"I need more than chips and nuts." Mike was sitting at the desk, already perusing the menu when his cell phone startled him.

"Who would be calling me at this hour?" He had to stand to retrieve the phone which was wedged in his front pocket. "Hmmm, private number. That could be anyone."

"Hello?"

"Hey Mike, don't let on to Jill that it's me."

Arnie whispered into the phone, as if someone were listening in on the other end in North Carolina. "Hello? Can you speak a little louder?" Mike wasn't sure of what he had heard.

"It's me, Arnie Kelly… but don't let on to Jill," he repeated.

"How are you two doing?"

"Fine, fine, and how are you?" Mike already felt uncomfortable.

"Listen. I have to be in New York next week. I'm giving a speech at a medical conference in the city. I was hoping to surprise Jill and drop in on her at SUNY. Thought she might have some time to show me around the medical school and the hospital, and maybe introduce me to some of the instructors. But I want it to be a surprise. Can you help me work it out?

"Oh! Um. I'm not even in New York right now. When are you coming?" Mike could feel a humming in his chest.

"Two weeks. I'll be there for the conference on Friday, and then will stay the weekend to spend some time with you kids." Arnie's voice was stronger now, resonating with delight in the fact that he would be able to see his Bean.

"Um, Arnie… I don't know what Jill's schedule is then… Um… I know she is doing a lot of weekends at the hospital and also some outside clinical rotations." Mike swallowed hard.

"Sometimes she is even upstate." Mike began pulling at his chin. "And me, I'm on tour for three more weeks. I sometimes can sneak home in the middle of the week if it's not too far."

"Oh, well, then I guess I'll have to work it out directly with Jill and forget about surprising her. I'll just call her at home." Arnie was about to end the phone call, but thought better of it. "So who are you traveling with, anyway?"

Mike gulped again. He was going to have to tell another lie. "It's just a small jazz combo. We are playing a bunch of small clubs around, trying to get a little more exposure. My usual gig is closed for renovations, so…"

"Sounds like fun. Think Jilly Bean is still awake?"

"Better call her in the morning. I know she has a quiet morning." Mike had now broken into a sweat. He felt extremely vulnerable, and found himself writing down exactly what he had told Arnie so he wouldn't forget his lie. "Arnie, I need to run. My posse is waiting for me."

"Okay buddy. Have a pleasant evening." Arnie placed the handset in its cradle tentatively, and stared over at the sound center in his den. Doris had gone to sleep and the house was painfully quiet. He reached down in the back of his record collection and pulled out his old copy of "Paradox Lost," and blew off the dust. He slid the album out of the ratty jacket and placed it carefully on his antiquated turntable. Turning the power on and the volume down simultaneously, Arnie then carefully dropped the needle on a particular song. He slid down into his recliner, used a remote to dim the lights, and lost himself in the song.

* * * * *

"Everything I've done so far; I've pulled off without a hitch. I'll figure something out. You don't even have to be involved." Jill leaned over, wrapped in a towel and used a second one to violently dry what was left of her hair. She had cut it short and dyed it orange to continue her transition from Jill Kelly to JayBee. Mike's reaction to her new look didn't matter to her. She had told him that he needed to be okay with what she had done, and that if what she looked like mattered more to him than how he felt about who she was on the inside, then maybe she was the wrong one for him.

"Yeah, baby, but I've already lied to him about this. How in the hell are you going to be in two places at one time?" Mike was wringing his hands, in between wiping his brow and bouncing his knee as he waited to hear her latest ruse. The knock at the door startled him.

"Let me get back in the bathroom. It's probably your food."

"Just put it on the desk, please." Mike fumbled for a couple of singles to tip the delivery boy.

"Thanks." Following him to the door, Mike closed it behind him, spun around and let Jill know it was okay to come out by knocking on the door. Bum bum Bum bum Bum bum.

"Cute." Jill was in a New York Giants jersey, ready for bed. "So after what she did for me tonight, Vee will shit a brick when I tell her I need to be in New York in two weeks. And when she asks why, I have to have a brilliant response." She flopped down across the bed, resting her head on her hands.

"This is all on you kiddo. I want no part of it."

Mike bit into his sandwich, keeping his back to her. He nearly choked on the first bite, his anxiety level peaking. Jill had been relaxed by the shower, but she, too, was feeling restless.

He's wrapped up in that sandwich. I can sneak in the bathroom with my purse. I'll have to put 'coming clean' on hold for now. Fuck. I gotta take this feeling away if I'm going to get through this one. Geez, Jill, there's always an excuse, always a reason.

"I'll be right back."

Mike didn't even look up. He was lost in thought, and trying to calm down as he forced the food down. The deeper the hole, the harder it was for him to function. He reached for the can of soda on the corner of the tray, and popping it open, he looked upward as if to pray.

The pill bottle was almost empty.

Shit! How many of these did I take tonight? This was supposed to last the whole fucking trip. Oh man. What am I gonna do? How can I get more? Oh well. Just one for now. That will at least take the edge off, and then maybe I can think.

"So, what if I tell Vee I have to go home because there's a family emergency? Do you think she'll buy that?" Jill emerged from the bathroom still holding the cup of water. "I only miss two concert dates that way, and then I can meet back up with you in Atlanta."

"Whatever."

"What, are you not going to help me anymore? We're almost there. I'm making enough money to live on; I just want to cut my first solo album. That's it."

Jill sensed that Mike was feeling defeated.

What was it he called it? Restless, irritable and discontent? That was a danger zone for him.

"Look, I love you, more than anything. I just need you to hold on for a few more months… maybe a year."

"I don't know if I can." Mike turned towards Jill. "I love you. I want us to be together, married, and building a life together. I want us to make music, and babies and a future. But this… this I cannot do anymore." Mike was no longer wiping perspiration from his brow. It was now tears from his eyes. "It's not like we can just part ways, either."

"What do you mean?" The Xanax was starting to work. Jill could feel the tension leaving her neck and shoulders.

"Part ways?"

"We are tied together by a contract, by a song, and by a deep emotion." Mike put the last corner of his sandwich down, and wiped his mouth with the napkin. He slid the chair clumsily back, getting the legs caught on the carpet. Standing, he turned toward Jill. "Here's how I feel. I want you to set a date for when this charade is going to be over. I want to know how you are going to do it, and I want to know that you will make it clear—abundantly clear, to your family, especially your father, that I had NOTHING to do with any of it. It was all you, and all I did was love you."

Disarmed, Jill collapsed her arms and rested her head across them.

"Wow! I wasn't expecting that." Her thoughts were racing.

I have no idea how and when I'm going to get out of this. While I know I wanted to at least release my first album, I don't have a timeline on when, and I definitely don't know how. I've been doing this spontaneously from the very beginning. What makes him think I have a plan now? Oh, and I do love you too, Mike. I would never throw you under the bus intentionally.

She looked over at Mike. He hadn't moved. He stood in front of her, seemingly wilting before her eyes. "Oh, Mike, I don't know what to tell you."

"That kind of answers my question." Mike considered his next move for a second. "Well, here's my plan. First, I'm going to run downstairs and see if there's another room. I don't think I can stay with you tonight." He started slowly for the door.

"Wait, don't go."

"Nothing more to say for now. You have some decisions to make and some actions to take. By the way, just so you know. I spoke for a few minutes with Vee, and she did tell me I could tell you this."

He presented the next sentence as if it were a board meeting, rather than a loving couple sharing good news.

"She's been scheduling for her next tour. Yes, we both have places on the tour, however instead of you singing just your one song with her, she wants you to do a full set and open for her next season."

Jill leapt to her feet.

"You're kidding!" She bolted toward Mike with her arms spread to hug him, but he stepped away.

"Is that enough for you?

Can't that be enough for you to divulge your secrets?"

Hurt by his evading her hug, Jill got surly.

"You know what? Go. Go get your other room. I just told you what my plan was. Apparently, that wasn't enough. Stop pushing. It's going to happen on my timeline, not yours."

Mike turned on his heels and was gone.

Jill collapsed on the bed, confused as to how she should feel.

Opening for Venus is the chance of lifetime, but at what cost? And will she still offer it to me if I bow out next week for a 'family emergency?' I can't breathe. This collar is too tight. Why didn't I bring by Jets jersey to sleep in. That, at least, is a vee neck. Ha ha... a "vee" neck. Where the hell is Mike going anyway? He'll be back. Shit. Mike come back, I can't breathe. I need to go to the hospital. What if Arnie calls now? What should I tell him? I need another pill. And I was going to tell him about the pills. Now he won't even stay with me. What happens if I wake up dead? That sounded ridiculous.

But I don't remember how many I took backstage. Shit.

Chapter 17

I knew I would know enough people to figure out a way to get a temporary ID. The key will be not to let Daddio get too close a look at it.

Jill stood in line at the grocery store with a few things to make it look like she and Mike had been home for the past two months.

I'll pour half of the milk out and some of the other stuff in the garbage in case he looks in the refrigerator. I'll dump some clothes in the hamper. I need to get a newspaper, too, to throw all over the kitchen table. What else? His conference is over in two hours.

"Hi Daddio!"

"Hey Bean! Funny, you hadn't called me that for years and suddenly you do it all the time!" Arnie was calling from midtown Manhattan, so he wasn't too far away from the newer apartment.

"Can you pick me up at the train in about an hour?"

"Sure! Where are you?"

"I'm at your school! Where are you?"

"I'm at home. I don't have any classes, labs or clinic today."

Can I make this work?

"I would have had to be down there for a lab, but the instructor had to be out of town on a family emergency."

That sounds familiar.

"I actually have the day off today. A whole day off!"

"Well why don't you come down here and show me around a little bit? I'd really like to meet some of your teachers and see the place." Arnie's interest in Jill's journey into medicine had waned since Eric was back in North Carolina for his residency.

"Dad, you know…. I'd really rather not. I don't really even know too many people in the cardiology department. And I know how you feel about my choices. I was hoping you would come uptown to see our apartment and maybe we could go to a museum or something." She was depending on the fact that he had been so wrapped up in the fact that Eric would soon be a full-fledged cardiologist, that he had only shown a modicum of enthusiasm for Jill's studies. OB/GYN was a waste of her talent, he thought, and they had fought enough about it. She was happy, so he should be happy.

"Okay, Bean, if that's how you'd rather spend the time. I've made arrangements to fly home in the morning, anyway." He glanced down at his watch.

"I can make it up there for a late lunch if you want. Just tell me where to meet you."

"It's fairly easy. Should only take you about thirty minutes or so this time of day." Jill dropped her shoulders.

Another crisis averted. I can probably get down to Mobile in time for tomorrow night.

"Get off at the Lincoln Square station. You only have to make one transfer."

"Whoa, Mike must really be doing well. That's Central Park West, isn't it?"

"He is doing really well, Dad. I think he's ready to cut his first album. I'll tell you all about it over lunch." Jill hung up the phone, at first feeling relieved, but within minutes, while she was putting the finishing touches on the lived in look of her apartment, she started to feel those ants crawling under her skin again. She stopped what she was doing, stood silently and began to pray. She had seen Mike do it a thousand times. She, however, had no idea how to pray.

Do I say God please get me through the next 24 hours without Dad finding out my secret? Or do I pray for this fucking anxiety to go away? Or what. WHAT???

Once again, she found herself rummaging through first her purse, and then the small plastic bag she had hidden under the pillow in the bedroom before she left.

Nothing. Not one pill.

Jill collapsed on the new couch they had delivered just prior to leaving on tour. She hugged herself and began rocking back and forth.

What have I done to myself? I don't just want that fucking pill. I now NEED it. I need the pill so I can see my own father. My father, who has no earthly idea what I've been up to for the last six and a half year. Oh God, help me. Help me. Well, I guess that's how I'm supposed to pray!

Her cries became verbal, no longer imprisoned between her ears. It began with a weep and grew steadily into a raspy sob. Soon Jill was gasping for breath and so absorbed in her convulsions that she didn't hear the phone ringing at first. When she was able to compose herself, even a little, she heard the jingle she had set for voice mail.

Jill dragged herself up to a standing position, and reached for her phone which was sitting precariously on the edge of the coffee table. She could barely see the number of the call she missed through her bleary, swollen eyes. It was Mike. She hesitated before pushing the redial button.

Gotta get a hold of myself so he can't hear me like this. I was gonna tell him. I was.

"Hey, sorry, I was in the bathroom."

"Hi baby. I've been thinking about you all morning."

Mike began by apologizing. He always did that, even if he wasn't wrong.

Jill knew that he hated having discord in his relationships, so he would often back down by saying 'I'd rather be at peace then be right. That's why it's not worth the fight.' Jill figured that was another one of his NA rules.

"Me too. I'm picking Dad up at the train in about fifteen minutes. I convinced him that I didn't want to go in to school on the one day off that I had." She paused, quizzically.

"Funny, I was surprised how easy that was. Anyway, he's leaving early in the morning, so I'm going to meet you all in Mobile."

"Oh, that's great. I'll let Vee know." There was a long silence before Mike continued. "We still have some talking to do, you know."

"I know." *You have no idea.*

"After Mobile we have a few days before we set up for Atlanta. We're doing two separate venues there so it's complicated. Doesn't pay to come home in between, so it's good you're coming back to tour tomorrow."

"Yeah, I really can't wait." Jill sat back down, this time all the way back on the couch, noticing that they left half of the plastic on across the back. "Listen, I have a few little things to do around here before I go get the Daddio. I'll call you later, okay?"

"Love you, Jill. I do."

"I love you, too."

Jill hung up the phone and stood quietly, mentally checking off her list the things she had to be sure of before she left to pick up her father. She scanned the apartment.

Everything looks lived in. Frig is full, clothes are strewn. Definitely looks like we're living here and busy. Oh wait. Medical books.

She darted into the bedroom and opened the closet door. In the back on the floor was a box of second-hand medical books she had purchased for just this occasion. Pulling out the Pharmacology books and a couple used notebooks, she returned to the dining room table and scattered them haphazardly.

That should do it!

Taking one last glance around and satisfied that all was in place, Jill picked up her purse, took a peek at herself in the mirror and stopped cold. "MY HAIR!" She had forgotten about her orange hair. Once again, she dropped her purse and went back to the rear of her closet. She dug through the cartons on the other side, hidden by the unpacked boxes from her last apartment. "There it is. My saving grace. Daddio never would have understood orange hair."

Carefully opening the box, Jill slid out the human hair wig, or sheitel as they called it at the wig store. She brushed her hair back as tightly as she could, and carefully fitted the wig on her head.

Looks just like my own hair used to. Unbelievable what those Orthodox Jewish women can do with these things. And Mike didn't want me to do it. "I'm so glad I did!" She smiled at herself in the mirror, drop-kicked the box into the coat closet, and was out the door.

* * * * *

The waiter placed the platter in front of Arnie, who was almost salivating by the time it arrived. "I think it's been a year since I had a good slab of beef. Your mother is driving me crazy, and now that Eric is home, I have two watchdogs." Arnie picked up the steak knife and fork and dug in.

Jill had a small salad in front of her. She also had a glass of cabernet. She had downed half of the wine and motioned the waiter for a second glass.

"What's this? You're drinking so early in the afternoon?" Arnie spoke with his mouth full.

He showed some concern about his daughter's drinking but it was overshadowed by his epicurean enjoyment.

"Had a rough night last night in clinic. It was very stressful. Just trying to take the edge off and enjoy my one day off, that's all."

Just trying to get rid of the ants in my legs, Dad. I ran out of pills… you have a better suggestion?

"You need some meds to help you sleep at night? Or maybe something for stress and anxiety?" Arnie put another large bite of steak in his mouth and began chewing. "I can write you a script."

"You know, Dad, that might just help." *Xanax, please.*

"Like what? I mean, I've been taking the pharmacology series at school. I don't want to get addicted to anything."

"It's true you have to be careful with the benzodiazepines, but if you're careful, I don't see why some Ativan or maybe Xanax would hurt." He patted his breast pocket. "I happen to have a prescription pad on me. You should be able to fill it at a national chain drugstore even though it's an out of state Drug ID. Remember, it's a controlled substance."

Don't I know it!

"Okay, thanks, Dad. But relax. After lunch." Jill picked at her salad with her fork, slowly managing to eat a little.

"So, how's Ivan doing?

"He actually made manager. He finally moved out to an apartment. It's in a singles complex, so he's making some friends, and he's even dating someone your mother approves of!"

"Wow! Now that's impressive."

"He still brings his laundry over for her to do for him. I think that will go on until he gets married." Arnie laughed out loud. Jill was taken aback by how relaxed her father was. Everything he used to bristle about, he seemed to be accepting.

Maybe Mike was right. Maybe the sooner I tell him, the better off we will all be. Maybe I can stop feeling so anxious. Maybe Mike and I will stop fighting.

"So, Dad…"

"Yes?" Arnie was wiping his mouth with a napkin with one hand, and reaching for his water with the other.

"You know how I didn't want to go into cardiology, and do you remember how upset you were with me?" Jill, once again, could feel her pulse in her ears. The pounding was deafening.

"I remember." He put the napkin down and gazed directly into his daughter's eyes. "It wasn't that long ago."

"Well…" She was bewildered. No words would come.

"Well, what?" Arnie could tell Jill had something to say. He waited.

"Um,"

"What, Bean? What's on your mind?"

"Uh… nothing really, I was just going to say that it seems like you've really mellowed."

I'm a chicken. I can't do this. I'm never going to be able to deal with this. Why is he still staring at me? Didn't I say enough to satisfy him?

Jill squirmed in her chair and reached for her wine. She took a big swallow. "Just that you used to blow your stack at Ivan for doing stuff like bringing his laundry, or me not following your path."

Arnie took another sip of water and carefully put the glass down. "I think it started to happen when we lost DeeGee." He dropped his head. "I miss him, and if I learned one thing from my father, and the way he lived his life, it was that happiness is not a destination. It is a journey. What I wanted for you was not necessarily going to make you happy; it was only going to make me happy."

"Wow, Dad, that's quite a revelation."

Maybe? Should I? I can't. I need Mike.

"DeeGee was a wise man." Jill sat back in her chair. She wasn't sure if it was the wine, the prospect of getting more of her Xanax or the fact that her Daddio was softening up as he got older.

She just knew, at that moment, that she was going to be able to pull this whole thing off.

"Whattaya say we blow off the museum, go back and see your apartment and maybe play a little music together, like we did when you were little." Arnie motioned for the check.

"By the way, Bean, I noticed your hair is a little darker than it used be. Are you not getting any sun up here?"

Jill sat there awestruck. First, that he noticed her hair, and second that they hadn't done this in at least ten years. When she reached high school, it seemed like Arnie never had time. He always wanted her studying or doing the hospital volunteer work. He had an intensity about school and was almost repulsed by the idea of playing and singing together.

"Yeah, Dad. I do a lot of studying and a lot of time in the hospital. You know what Daddio? I think would just love that! It's been forever since we sang together."

But first can we stop at the pharmacy?

* * * * *

Jill tossed around in the seat of the plane, often elbowing the passenger to her left. She absolutely hated flying economy class. She had been spoiled flying on Vee's private plane. It was so roomy. There were even places to lie down and nap if it was a long enough flight. She finally sat up and reached for the flight attendant call button. While she waited, she pulled the small bottle of pills out of her jacket pocket, and, opening it, she shook two out into her hand.

It won't hurt to take two now. I only had one before takeoff. I'll be able to get my shit together before Mike picks me up. Or was

I supposed to Uber to the hotel. Shit, I don't remember, now. Great, now I can't remember things. What the hell did he say? Oh wait; maybe it was a text conversation.

"Dammit!" The pills slipped out of her hand while she tried to pry her phone from the other pocket of her jacket. Now the lady sitting next to her was getting irritated.

What are you looking at? Haven't you ever seen an addict craving dope? What's the matter, don't you like my hair? Did I say that out loud?

The flight attendant reached in and turned off the call light. "May I help you with something?

She seems pissed at me too. What did I do?

"May I have a small cup of water, please? I need to take some medication."

Did that sound normal? I feel like everyone is staring at me. Move along, the show's over.

"Certainly." The flight attendant disappeared down the aisle, while Jill tried desperately to retrieve the pills from the floor between her feet.

This is sinking pretty low. I really could just get some clean ones out of the bottle. But this has to last me for another nine days.

After swallowing the dirty pills, Jill curled up in a little ball on her seat, holding herself as tight as possible until the Xanax kicked in. Fifteen minutes later, whether it was from the medication or the exhaustion from the stress, Jill had finally fallen off to sleep.

* * * * *

"Just landed." Jill texted to Mike.

"Great. I'll drive around in about ten minutes. That should give you enough time to get to the arrival area. You didn't check anything, did you?"

Phew. "Nope. In fact, I left almost everything at home since the tour's almost over. That way I'll have more room for packing for the 'final' trip home."

She sent the text, but then decided to send another: "Can't wait to give you a hug. I love you."

Chapter 18

"Ladies and Gentlemen, Venus"

Same show they opened with in Chicago. Same set, same song list, and same costumes. The only difference was that Jill, or JayBee as everyone, even Mike was calling her, was now singing "I Can Feel Your Heart Beat" strictly as her own solo, with an incredible introduction from Vee.

"Good Evening Hot Lanta!" The crowd was untamed. The Philips Arena was packed. For the first time during the entire tour, Jill noticed that there was a huge contingency of gay fans. It didn't bother her. In fact, they were loyal fans to Vee, to Bette Midler, and so many other great stars and musicians. She wondered, though, if they were going to be her following as well.

The first number had gone well, but now it was time for JayBee to knock their socks off. Jill, however, was teetering. She had taken one too many pills from her bottle of Xanax and tossed them down her throat without water. It had been getting more and more difficult to find a minute alone. By the end of the tour everyone was so close; nobody ever had any time to themselves. She nearly stumbled to the middle of the stage when Vee announced her name. She was together enough to notice, though, that this Atlanta audience was ready and waiting for her. They cheered for her almost as loudly as they did for Vee.

"Thank you, thank you." The music kicked in. Her cue came and went. She was dazed, just glancing around the arena, astounded at how high it was.

Are all basketball arenas this high? Oh wait, I was supposed to start singing. Should I ask them to start over or just come in?

She turned halfway around to try to spot Mike, who had a panicked, questioning expression on his face as he tried to guide the band back to the opening without missing a beat. He nodded to Jill and she caught where he was.

"I can hear your heart beat… I can feel your heart feel, I can know your thoughts as if we were one…" That was close, she thought to herself. "I can know your thoughts as if we were one…" sang Jill, somehow able to finish the song with no more mistakes.

"Thank you Atlanta!"

Jill missed on only a few cues as the evening progressed, thankfully not on any of the solos.

She waded through the rest of her songs, dances and harmonies, praying to get to the end. The rest of the concert went off without a hitch, or so it seemed to the audience.

* * * * *

"Hey! What's your problem?" Vee motioned violently with her arms for Jill to join her in her dressing room. She was already in a pair of jeans and a tee shirt, yet Jill was milling around the back hallway, still in costume from the last number.

"Whaddaya mean?" She staggered toward the door. "I'm just really tired. I think the tour just sucked the life out of me."

"Oh really? So then are you telling me you don't want to join us on the next tour?" Vee was still angry about Jill's antics on stage. She had no patience for artists on her team that use or drink before or during a performance. "If you're stoned, you're out anyway, you know that right?" She met Jill at the door. "Look, I don't care a flying fuck what you do on your own time.

I don't even mind a little beer or wine while we rehearse, but you are NEVER to be compromised on stage ever again, you got it?"

"Yes ma'am." Jill spun around to leave, but lost her balance and fell. "Oooops!"

"Hey, JayBee, come in here a minute."

Jill scrambled to her feet and joined Vee in her dressing room, closing the door behind her.

"Is this a problem for you or is it a onetime deal. I need you to be honest with me. Cuz if it's a problem, I wanna help."

"Vee, I can't talk about it."

"Well, you need to talk to me about it, because I won't invest any more time and money in you if I don't know what I'm getting into, and you clearly were not right tonight."

"I need to talk to Mike first." She sat down silently on a chair in the corner as if were remanded to time out. "Do you have a minute?"

"We are not flying out until tomorrow, honey. I got all night."

"Yeah, but I don't." Jill began to weep. "Mike doesn't know it, but I somehow got myself hooked on benzos. Not only haven't I been able to stop, I've been using more and more. I've been afraid to tell him, because he has like six years clean, and he's really serious about his sobriety."

Jill couldn't believe she was actually telling on herself. "I want off. I just don't know how to do it without Mike finding out."

"Oh Honey, he's got to know. He's your fiancé, for God's sake." Vee sat cross-legged on the floor in front of Jill, rested her hands on her protégé's knees and looked up into her eyes. "He loves you. I know he only wants the best for you. You HAVE to tell him. In fact, he probably can really help you because he's already been through this himself."

"I can't." Jill began to sob.

"I'll help you tell him. I can stay with you." Vee stood up. "It's the very least I can do for my shining star. Let me go get him." She started for the door.

"Wait, no, I'm not ready."

"When will you be ready… when you're six feet under? I've watched this too many times." Vee poked her head out the door and yelled down the hall. "Send Mike Munoz in here right away, would ya?"

Jill sat very still, weeping quietly into her hands. Her body should slightly with tremors. She wasn't sure if it was from fear or if her body was telling her to take another pill. "This is when it happens. This is when I give in."

"What does that mean?" Vee returned to her spot on the floor.

"I don't know if what I'm feeling is because I need more pills or if I'm just scared. It seems like everything runs together in my head and in my body… like I've lost touch with what's real and what I'm imagining."

"What's up, boss." Mike knocked gently as he opened the door. As soon as he had it wide enough, he spotted Jill in the corner with Vee on the floor in front of her. His face lost all of its color "What's the matter? What happened?"

Vee stood back up as if to run interference. "Mike, JayBee is having a little problem. She needs for you to be gentle and kind and she needs you to help her. I'm here with both of you too, no matter what, okay?"

"Jill, what's happening, baby?" Mike rushed over to Jill and put his arms around her. "Your whole body is shaking. Did something happen?" He put two fingers under her chin and forced it up to look at her face. It was as if he was able to look right through her. "Oh man, what have you done to yourself?"

"I'm so sorry, Mike. I'm sorry." Jill couldn't bring herself to make eye contact. She tried to look away. "I've been taking some sedatives, for a while, now." She sat silently for what seemed like an eternity, but was able, finally, to finish the sentence. "…and now I can't stop."

"Is that what was going on with you on stage tonight?" Mike spoke softly.

"Yeah, I guess I took too much before the show. I really fought to stay centered and focused. Only really messed up on the solo, but my mind… I was all over the place." Jill started sobbing again. "I need help."

"Holy." Mike just held her again, pulling her closer. "It'll be okay. We'll get through this together." He sat with her, gently rubbing her back and holding her head in place with his other hand. "We'll take you over to a detox center, and we'll get you under control. And then we're going to get rid of those demons that are causing the anxiety."

Vee backed away, slowly. "Hey, guys, please tell me this isn't because I pushed you too hard and too fast; because if I did, I'm so, so sorry." She earnestly scanned both of their faces to try to read the answer to her question. Mike and Jill didn't even hear the question. Vee asked in a different way.

"Were you not ready to solo? Did I put too much pressure on you?"

Jill reacted to this question. "Oh no, please, Vee, it has nothing to do with that. I was ready, and I can't begin to tell you how much I appreciate the opportunity."

"No, Jill has a much bigger issue to deal with." Mike made her look him in the eye this time.

"But let's do one thing at a time. Let me get you some water." Hesitantly, he let go of her and turned to Vee.

"Can you stay a few minutes while I get her something to drink?"

"There's some mineral water in the fridge in the other corner."

"Thanks." Mike almost lunged across the room and grabbed a bottle from the small refrigerator.

He opened it and handed it to Jill. He then found another chair and slid it over to sit next to her. While she was slowly sipping on the water, Mike scanned his phone for nearest hospital that had a detox unit.

"There's a Wellstar Hospital nearby. We can go over there. They have an inpatient medical detox unit. However long it takes, we stay in the Atlanta area, and then we'll go home and get you started on a recovery program."

"Hold on." Jill was shaking her head. "You think it's that bad?"

"Detoxing from benzos is the worst, my friend. The worst. If you don't do it with some help, you're going to be miserable. Otherwise it will take you forever, a tiny, tiny bit at a time."

Vee chimed in. "You can't do it yourself. Besides, we don't have time for you to do that. I need you ready for rehearsals in two months. We go back on the road in four months, and I want you with us." She then mouthed something to Mike, who nodded his head.

"JayBee, or Jill, or whatever your name is… I know Mike told you about my plans for you for next tour."

Jill nodded her head sleepily.

"So, are you in?"

Jill continued to nod her head, but was very drowsy, and ready to sleep off the night's festivities.

"Okay," Vee continued. "Then here's the new verbal agreement. You will go to medical detox. You will stay as long as the doctors deem necessary. You and Mike will return to New York and establish a recovery routine. He will see to it that you follow it by attending whatever meetings and groups you need to go to. Rehearsals begin in June. The cost you incur at this detox will be picked up by my company. Period, no discussion." She stepped back.

"Agreed?"

Jill was sound asleep. Mike asked if his word was good enough.

"I guess your word will have to suffice. Go. Take her.

You need a limo?" Mike shook his head no. "Okay then, call me first thing in the morning."

* * * * *

"Are you sure I'm not going to have any more of those seizures?"

The doctor stood in the doorway grasping the clipboard with both hands and scanning the night nurse's notes. "It's highly unlikely. I believe it's been two weeks since the last bout with any serious detox symptoms. You've been stable and we've been able to titer you down all of the meds. We can send you home with only one prescription, and that's the clonidine. Even that, you'll be off of soon enough." He flipped the papers back down.

"That's great, doc," said Mike. "So, when are you going to discharge her. I want to make airline reservations."

"You can go tomorrow, I think." The doctor smiled, slipped out of the doorway and let the door slowly close behind him.

"Honey, that's terrific." Jill lay in the bed and stared off in the distance.

"Jill, you there?" Mike was surprised at the lack of happiness or any emotion she was expressing.

"I'm a little scared."

"Perfectly normal." Mike paused in reflection. "I remember that feeling."

"No, I mean, I'm not scared of leaving the hospital and going back to New York. I'm scared of doing the next thing."

"What, getting into a recovery routine?"

"I thought you were going to make me tell my family about my double life."

"Jill, if there's one thing I know, your recovery has to come first. They say anything you put before your recovery, you're gonna lose." He shook his head as if he were agreeing with himself. "Seen it happen over and over again. Not letting that happen to you… Or I should say I'm going to help you to help yourself, so that you won't let that happen."

So, I can go forward with my original plan… I will reveal to my family who JayBee is AFTER I release my own album. And I really have to stop talking to myself.

"Phew!" Okay, then I'm ready to rock and roll." Jill extended her arms wide, inviting Mike over to hug him. "Hey, do you think maybe we could sneak downstairs for some ice cream?"

"I have a better idea. They only have those little ice cream cups or Nutty Buddies down there. How about if I find us some Edy's Ice Cream?"

"Great. You know what kind."

* * * * *

Jill pulled the hospital tray over to her and pulled out her music composition book. She had, in the time she was hospitalized, been able to crank out six songs. She was planning on asking Vee if she could do one of them on tour in her opening act along with Heart Beat and a few cover songs, and the others she was going to present to Mike as her beginning work toward that first album. Her only problem was that there was no place to work on the music in privacy. There was a piano in the detox lounge, and there was one on the second floor lobby lounge of the main hospital. Neither one afforded her the chance to bang out a tune or work out harmonies and chords, while stopping in between to write things down, change lyrics or syncopation. A most difficult creative environment, her detox experience did, at least, give her myriad ideas for new songs. And the sounds inside a hospital inspired a whole new rhythm in her head.

* * * * *

"Be it ever so humble…" Jill started to sing.

"Hey, that could be a song." Mike held the apartment door open with his foot while Jill carried his two saxophones and her overnight bag in. He followed with the large roller suitcase and his overnight bag. He got as far as the foyer, stopped cold and wrinkled his nose. "What the hell is that smell?"

"Oh geez, oh no." Jill put her hand to her forehead.

"I forgot. I had brought in a bunch of food when I was home to see Dad, fully expecting to be home in ten days. I guess it all went bad in the fridge." She walked gingerly into the kitchenette, and pulled at the refrigerator door. The suction was strong as it had been closed tight for three and a half weeks; however the smell that emanated was strong throughout the apartment. "Do I really want to open this?"

"I'll take care of it. I want you to go into the outside pocket of my tote bag. There's a list of meetings." Mike was stoic.

"Pick one."

"I haven't even unpacked yet and you're starting?"

"I'm continuing. You can't stop now." He left the roller back in at the edge of the carpet in the dining room and joined her in front of the refrigerator. Taking her arms with his hands, he looked her straight in the eyes and went on. "This is an action program. Anytime you are not moving forward, and that includes standing still… you're moving backwards. Don't undo all of the good you did in Atlanta."

Jill began to pull away, but he wouldn't let her. He held her in place, and then pulled her close to him, pressing her against him. Her head rested against his chest. She heard that familiar sound… the sound that started it all.

It had been the beginning of their friendship, the beginning of their romance, the start of their partnership, and the very sound that would soon launch her solo career.

She thought back to the first night the beat came to her, while she tried unsuccessfully to study for a microbiology test. The lies had already started. The subterfuge had been in motion for a while by then.

What took me so long to succumb to the pressure? I never lied to my parents as a kid. In fact, I had been the model child; I was the straight "A" student; I was active in the church; I volunteered at the nursing home.... Oh wait, no I didn't... I was already lying to them by then.

"Now go, do what I suggest, and I'll get rid of the culprit or culprits in the refrigerator, and then we'll go to a meeting together." Mike let go of her, noticing that familiar look in her eyes. She was dazed, lost in thought. "Jill, come on. Focus on your recovery here."

"Yeah, okay." She pushed away and fumbled through Mike's bag to find the list. "Hey, are they all at churches?" She scanned the list quickly. "It makes me uncomfortable going into a church about this stuff."

"A lot are, but we can find some free-standing places or some in other places if you want."

Mike was holding his nose with one hand and dumping, one at a time, several items in the refrigerator that had turned either sour, or a color that was clearly not normal for the food that was marked on the label. "Some of this stuff would have been fine if you hadn't opened it six weeks ago."

"I had to make it look authentic."

"Yeah, well, once you unfold all of this to your family, and work your steps, you're going to have a whole new understanding of what it means to live authentically, honey." Mike smirked as he tied the plastic bag. "I'm going to run this down the hall to the trash chute. Be back in two minutes, and then we can go."

"Right now?"

"When is a better time to dive in?" He was gone.

Jill shrugged her shoulders. For a split second, she thought she might have left some pills hidden in the bedroom, but then remembered she had taken them the day her dad was in town. "Not home for a minute and I'm already looking for them. Wow. I'm a sick puppy."

She glanced over to the front door, hoping Mike hadn't heard her when she realized she had said that out loud.

Guess that's better than saying it to myself inside my head.

"Okay, let's roll." Mike grabbed his jacket, and rolled the suitcase up against the wall. He extended his hand to Jill. "I'm with you all the way. Let's go get some recovery."

* * * * *

"My name is Jill and I'm an addict." Jill stood tentatively. She didn't know a soul in this room besides Mike, but he seemed to know everyone. "I have thirty-three days clean. I'd just like to listen today, thanks for letting me share." She sat down.

Phew, glad that's over.

Mike stood up and shared. Jill was in a panic, thinking he was going to talk about all that happened in Atlanta. He spoke about how important it was that while he was on tour, he found meetings in cities all over the country, and even when he didn't know anyone, he felt comfortable and safe, that his clean time would be protected as long as he stayed close to the program. Jill sat back and listened to others tell their stories, some of them hopeful, some of them really sad. The hour seemed to fly by. When they reached the end, two girls came over and gave her their phone numbers. "Call anytime."

"They're pretty nice." Jill admitted to Mike that the experience wasn't nearly as horrible as she had anticipated, but she had no desire to go for coffee with those women.

"That's okay. I think you'll get more comfortable as you go to more meetings." Mike reached for her hand as they walked to the car. He spoke no more of the meeting. "We have some unpacking to do, and some laundry to do. And we need to get some fresh food in the place."

"*We* have all that to do?" Jill was surprised by Mike's offer to participate in getting up and running again upon their return. His interest in the day-to-day workings of life at home had always been slim or none. "Okay, what would you like to tackle first?"

"First, let's go grab a bite and then go to the grocery store."

"Sounds like a good plan. I could eat an elephant." Mike started to react but before he could, she added, "I know, one bite at a time."

Chapter 19

"Here's how it's going to work." Vee had a load of paperwork on the desk in front of her, and Vick, her agent sat to her left. Mike and Jill sat across the table facing them. "I'm not too happy about letting you go, because I love you, you know that, right?"

"Letting me go?" Jill was horrified. "You mean I'm fired? We're not going to join you on the tour?" Jill took a deep breath and swallowed hard. "Vee, I've been clean for over three months, and we've been going to meetings every day. This is no longer an issue, I promise."

"Cool your jets, Jilly Bean." Vee interrupted, before Jill exploded completely.

"I used the wrong expression; in fact, I don't even know what cool your jets means or where it came from." She jumped up from her chair and hustled around to the other side of the table, wrapping her arms around her little star. "I meant I don't want to 'launch you into a solo career' letting you go. You have so much natural given talent and such an intense stage presence." She released the hug.

"We have a plan we'd like to propose for you."

Returning around to her seat, Vick took over. "Look, honey. Vee recognizes greatness when she sees it. You won't fly right away on your own, so she's offering you an extraordinary opportunity." Vick took the top stack of papers and spun it around so it was facing Jill and Mike. "Vee would like to offer you the chance to open for her, an exclusive twenty-minute spot, before every show on her upcoming tour. You will have to provide your own content, which she will have to approve and you won't be able to do covers of any of her music."

Jill's jaw dropped as she stared at the contract. She was speechless. She tried to focus on the numbers at the top to determine the length of the contract. There was nothing on the top page about compensation, but she didn't want to seem too eager. "Uhhh, ohh my."

Mike was very quiet. He waited for someone to make the next move.

Vick continued. "This is a contract for this tour only. Anything for the future will have to be renegotiated." He slid his finger down the page. "Here are the dates for the tour, and the cities.

It's slightly longer than last winter's tour." He then picked up the contract and flipped to the next page.

"As far as compensation goes, we are offering you the same salary as you were making."

"Wait, what?" Jill was obviously confused. "Shouldn't I make considerably more money now?"

Vick sat back in his chair and started to laugh.

"They always think it's about the money, don't they Vee?"

Vee reached over and took the contract back. "JayBee, let me explain." She took a sip of her tea and began," You are getting an intangible gift here. Nobody can really estimate the value of what I'm offering you here. The prospect of playing before my fans is something you can't put a price on." Vee sat back in her chair.

"Now! You can do this, you can remain as a back-up singer on the tour, or you can strike out on your own. You decide."

So, who peed in your cornflakes this morning? Why are you being so bitchy about it? I just asked a question.

"I don't want to sound like I don't appreciate it, because you know I do," Jill began. "But I need to talk all of this over with Mike. And you haven't said anything about him and what his role will be. And do I have the use of your musicians or do I have to bring my own band? I mean, I have an awful lot of questions."

Vee was tired. She had been out in California doing a benefit taping. She yawned. "Okay, I get it. Let me know your decision as soon as you've made it, but certainly before rehearsals start, okay." She got up and left the conference room, allowing the door to slam behind her.

Vick threw his head back. "Don't mind her. She's probably having her period."

"Excuse me?" Jill never liked Vick, and it was probably because of comments like that. "I really don't appreciate sexist comments like that. Think Vee would like knowing you said that?"

"You threatening me honey?"

"I'm not your honey, either. My name is Jill, or JayBee.

But I'm NOT your honey, your sweetie or your doll." Jill stood up abruptly, snatched a copy of the contract and left in the same way Vee had.

Vick's eyes met Mike's, looking for some sort of validation. Mike just shook his head, picked up a copy of the contract and turned to leave. Bra-burn

"You too? Don't tell me you're one of those feminist bra-burners, too." Vick sneered at Mike.

Mike was just about to open the door when he turned around. He inhaled, deeply. "I'm not going to even justify that with a reaction. But just do yourself and all of us a favor. Keep your stupid mouth shut when we're around, okay? You don't want to mess with this feminist."

* * * * *

Jill was already waiting downstairs in the foyer. Vee had disappeared into the south side of the house, her residence, so she hadn't had a chance to talk further. She paced back and forth waiting for Mike to come down. Peeking into the living room, she spotted a tall cabinet in the corner. It had floor to ceiling glass panes and glass shelves. It was lit with tiny spotlights only on the contents, which were not a surprise to Jill.

Sitting on each shelf were two Grammy Awards. *That's three shelves, two on each. Geez, the woman has six Grammies and she hasn't even turned thirty yet. Who am I to question her?*

"Let's get out of here." Mike had come up behind Jill, startling her. "I think I've had about enough of this operation for one day."

"Wait, Mike. Look in there."

Mike was in no mood to be delayed, but to appease Jill, he stopped and poked his head around the corner.

"Nice, so what?"

"I think I'd be making a mistake not taking advantage of her offer, that's all. It's pretty clear she knows what she's doing in this crazy industry. And look beyond the case. I think those are Platinum Records or C-D's." She looked up at Mike. "Let's go home and look over the paperwork, and then talk it over, okay?"

"Fine."

"Hey, what's wrong?"

"Nothing, let's just go." Mike opened the front door, setting off the buzzer. The attendant (he got offended when they referred to him as the butler the first time they came), came out of the back and looked down the hall to see who was leaving. Mike tipped his imaginary hat to him and they left.

Walking to the car became an adventure for Jill as Mike's long legs, when moving fast, would force her into a light trot. "Slow down, Mike. We're out of there. What's the hurry?"

"I'm sorry. I just had to get out of there and away from that pig of a lawyer she has."

"Is that all that's bothering you? If it is, you need to let it go. You can't worry about what other people think, do, or say.

You can only be responsible for your reaction to it. Otherwise, he'll mess with your serenity."

"Boy, you sure talk a good program." He chuckled to himself. He knew she was right. "There's a little more we need to talk about, but let's just get going and talk on the way or when we get home. I want to miss rush hour if possible."

* * * * *

"So, what happens to me?" Mike picked up his glass of iced tea and took a long sip. "What happens to me when you leave Vee after this tour, and strike out on your own? Have you given that any thought?" Mike's face was somber. No, sober.

Jill crumpled back into her chair. Never once had she stopped to think about what Mike would do. She couldn't answer him.

"I mean, I don't want to stand in the way of your dreams." Silence. He stared blankly at the glass still in his hand. "I just always thought we were in this together… that we were a team."

Jill was motionless. She couldn't concentrate. "Oh Mike, I was so caught up in the excitement, I didn't even think that far ahead."

"It's not that far ahead."

"I know." Jill's breathing became rapid.

There's that terrible feeling again. Am I going to pass out again? Not drugs this time. Calm down. You're an adult. We can figure this out together.

"Hey, are you okay? You're pale."

"Yah, I'm just a little upset… with myself."

That was a lie. I'm not okay.

"We have to figure this out." Jill wiped her brow with the back of her hand.

"Do you need me to call nine eleven Jill? You're scaring me. Your lips are grey."

"I'll just sip on some cool water. I'll be okay." She took slow breaths through her nose and let them out carefully through her lips for a minute or two. It began to pass.

"Come on, let's go." Mike motioned for the check. "Let's get you home."

"Were you finished eating? Really, I'm okay now." She was. She got through it. No drugs, no passing out. The thumping in her chest had subsided. "We can go if you want."

"I'm through. I just would rather get you home, where we can just talk quietly."

Jill slowly stood up, sliding the chair back with her legs, keeping her hands on the table to maintain her balance. She really was okay.

I really am okay. I did it. I can get through that without the pills.

Jill and Mike left the café arm in arm, with Jill leaning ever so slightly on his strength to get her safely to the car. They drove home in silence. At least verbally. Her mind was racing.

He could be the basis or MY new band. He knows enough people to put together a new band. Would Vee hate me for stealing him? Nah, she'd understand. He's my fiancé, for God's sakes. Or he could at least help me audition musicians. Or maybe I won't jump after only one tour. That will give me a full year to write some songs and look around for musicians, maybe establish my own brand. I already have an idea for the name for my first album.

And I have to start putting together some plan for telling my family about all of this. Oh Geez, I need to call Mom and Dad. We have to go down to North Carolina for Eric's graduation. Oh man and I'm supposed to graduate next year. There's so much, TOO much to think about. See, this is when I need to quiet my mind. I can't handle this chaos between my ears. When we get home, I'm going to fix myself some warm milk and try to take a nap. That's should help.

* * * * *

"Hey, Jill, wake up." Mike gently shook Jill by the shoulders. "That's some deep sleep you're in." He tried again, and Jill began to stir.

"Oh hi, baby. What time is it?

"It's already seven." Mike sat down on the side of the bed next to her. "You only had the milk, right?"

Jill sat up with a start. She did not hold back her anger. "You were with me every minute of the day. What do you think?"

"I'm sorry. I had to ask. You were sleeping for almost four hours."

"You didn't have to ask. You could have trusted me and trusted in the fact that I might just be tired."

"Jill. Remember that I've been where you are right now. I know it's not easy, so it wouldn't be a surprise, with all that's happened today, if you gave in to the temptation. I just wanted to be sure you were okay. Remember, I'm on your side, not against you."

"I know, I'm sorry. No, I'm clean… I was just exhausted from all of the excitement. And worried," she added.

"Worried about what?"

"I was worried about you and how we're going to go forward."

"I was thinking about it. I have some good ideas, but I need to go uptown. Remember, I'm playing at that little club tonight." He started to get up, but then added, "You want to join me?"

"Nah, but thanks. I think I better stay home and rest. Maybe I'll fool around with some melodies or lyrics. If this is going to happen, I need to get to work. Or I should say *we* need to get to work." She swung her legs over the side of the bed and slipped her feet into her shoes. "Can you pull down the keyboard from the top of the closet before you go?"

"Sure." Mike went into the closet and pulled down their old Yamaha keyboard. "I think it's time we replace this with a bigger one."

He set it up in the bedroom since there are no neighbors that share that wall. "Good luck writing."

"Good luck playing. Love you, Baby."

* * * * *

"Okay, so if we eliminate 'Don't Ever,' and add in the cover of 'Million Reasons' by Lady Gaga, it will time out perfectly. That way, there's only one cover, and the rest is original stuff.

What do you think?" Jill had been actually trying to figure all of the timing without using a calculator.

Mike sat on the stool in Vee's studio swiveling back and forth laughing. "You are too funny."

"What did I say that was so funny?" Jill was never more focused and serious. "This has to be perfect."

"Vee is going to laugh at you too, you know." Mike was now doing full spins on the stool. "It doesn't have to time out exactly to twenty minutes, for one. And two, you didn't allow one second for audience reaction. Hopefully, the crowd will go wild."

He put his hands to his mouth as if to yell and blew his breath loudly through the opening, mimicking the sound of a large bunch of spectators cheering uncontrollably.

Jill blushed. For the first time, she was humbled by the position in which she now found herself. Vee had been coaching her on her music content, her stage presence and her dance steps. She had even given her a few pointers on branding herself. She needed to make a statement and stick to it so her fans could always identify her music, her message and her look. She had come such a long way in such a short time. The best part was the arrangement she had allowed for Mike.

"He's the best in the business right now." Vee didn't hold anything back. "I want to keep him with me but as we've been hearing a lot lately, love trumps all, and since you two can't keep your hands off each other, even at rehearsal. For God sakes, get a room."

Vee had agreed to let Jill use her band through the tour, and Mike was free to leave, if he wanted, when the tour was over, but he had to sign a non-compete clause in his contract. He got a raise for doing both shows, but he was not permitted to woo any other musicians away from her band when he went about the business of putting together JayBee's band. They all had multi-year contracts as a result of this whole arrangement, with built in raises, so they were all thrilled.

"Vee is going to be perfectly fine with your song list, Jill. So, can we get her down here to review it so we can go home? I'm exhausted." Mike glanced down at his watch. It was after eight o'clock, and while rush hour was over, this was his only night off the whole week. He wanted to go home and sleep. "We start regular rehearsals on Monday.

You're gonna be sick of this studio by the time the tour starts."

"I'll have them call her and ask her to come down." Jill picked up the intercom and called the attendant. He then relayed the message to Vee's private residence.

Ten minutes later, Vee appeared in her bathrobe and a turban towel on her head. "I was just about to climb into bed to watch a movie. I had no idea you two were even still here."

"I didn't mean to disturb your private time. I just wanted you to approve my song list, per our contract."

Vee snatched the list from Jill's hand. Jill could see the eye movement as Vee scanned the paper. "Looks great. It may end up being a little long, that is, if they love you. And they will.

Be prepared to do an encore, okay? Good night." She turned on the heels of her bedroom slippers and almost skipped from the room. She tossed one last comment over her shoulder on the way out. "Now go home and get some rest. We have a long four months ahead of us. After that, I expect a wedding invitation and then an invite to make a cameo appearance on your first album."

She vanished.

* * * * *

"This is just what I had hoped it would be like. It's nothing like what I had dreamed when I sang into my brush in front of the mirror in my bedroom as a kid; or when I sat next to my dad at the piano; or when I starred in the church Christmas pageant." Jill finished loading her equipment in the trunk and Mike had commandeered the back seat for his equipment.

"Think we're going to have to break down and buy a mini-van or something. I imagined all of the glamour of the spotlights, but forgot about this part."

"What part do you mean?" Mike finished up and slammed the door. The old Chevy was still holding up, but he saw Jill's point and was ready to part ways with his car.

"I mean the loading, the lifting; the late nights; the songwriting. It's really a lot of grunt work that goes on to put together a show. I guess I never really appreciated how hard these guys work." She stopped for a second. "I used to really resent some of these rap artists. You know the ones I mean; the guys that started out rapping on the street corners, with no real musical training, who were able to take what they called music to the market place, and make it really big. They have the same number of Grammies as Vee has, but with no formal training. Now I see, though, that they do have to put in a lot of hard work."

* * * * *

"Ladies and gentlemen, opening for Venus tonight is a singer who she introduced on her tour last year. Please put your hands together tonight for JayBee!"

The flashes of lights around the arena were exactly as she had asked. They resembled, to a tee, the lights as they used to dance across the ceiling of her bedroom back home in North Carolina. This was not done necessarily to comfort her, other than to remind her that this was the last stop to her dream coming true. The light show began to change colors as she entered the stage from the back, a spotlight following her from above. The drums started a slow steady beat, a familiar one. This was her sense of comfort. Bum bum Bum bum Bum bum….

"I can hear your heart beat… I can feel your heart feel, I can know your thoughts as if we were one…"

They like it. And it's me they like. They all know the song. I have to focus. Let loose, Bean. Give this everything you've got. This first performance won't make or break me, but it will make an impact. I'll probably get a review. Will I get a review? There has to be somebody in the audience who will do a review. Sing, dammit.

"I can know your thoughts as if we were one…"

This is really happening. I'm doing it. Yay me. Stop patting yourself on the back and sing…

Chapter 20

The clinking of ice in glasses and a dull hum of whispering was all that floated up to the scaled down stage. Jill didn't refer to this as a crowd, this time. It was an audience. It was an intimate, friendly group of her followers. The tour was on its last stop, this time in Las Vegas. Vee had scheduled two concerts. This one was in one of the hotels, in a small lounge, and they were playing to the high rollers, a bunch of Vee's friends and family, and many celebrities, including their usual groupies and paparazzi.

I'm okay with this. I have to be. We rehearsed the smaller version of the production numbers for Vee's show, and cut back on the numbers of my singers and dancers. This will work fine.

Jill peeked out from the side curtain one more time. "It's nice when the thoughts between my ears are positive." She spoke very softly, but was startled when Kenny tapped her on the shoulder from behind.

"Ya got about three minutes, JayBee." Kenny pushed past her and went out on stage to his little corner, and started fiddling with some of the dials on his sound board, listening carefully for any signs of feedback or crackles. His equipment had suffered some at the last venue and it hadn't been perfect at rehearsal.

Jill stepped back away and turned to look in the mirror one more time. "You Gotta Have Heart… Sing Out Louise… Project and Enunciate… but most of all, have fun."

Vee was now standing behind her. "What the hell was that all about? I know I never know where sayings come from, but that was weeeeeeird."

"A couple of lines from some Broadway Shows, a drama teacher and something my Dad always said to me right before I went on stage." Jill smiled, thinking to herself that it wouldn't be long before she could share all of this with her Daddio. "Well, I got a show to do…"

The lights came up slowly. The crowd was silent. Kenny had stopped introducing Jill three weeks ago. The protocol was now that she would enter, sing "I Can Feel Your Heart Beat," and when the audience quieted down, she would introduce herself by saying, "Good Evening," or "Hey there," or something like that, and then, "I'm JayBee… let's rock out!" She had tried not to mimic Vee. She was trying to establish her own brand, and her music was a little more rock and roll rather than pop.

Here I go… She launched into her new song, "To Thine Own Self." The audience gave it a lukewarm reception. *It takes time, Jilly Bean, It takes time.*

* * * * *

Sitting on a plush couch in the green room after the show, Mike and Jill watched all of the people coming and going, congratulating Vee, staying for a few minutes for a quick glass of wine and then making their way out to the casino or to another show.

Mike leaned in to Jill and whispered, "I have a silly idea."

"Most of your ideas are silly."

Mike wrinkled up his face. "Let's go get married."

Jill didn't even look at him. "You're right. That is a silly idea."

"Why not? We're in Vegas, we have the time, and we have all of our friends here."

It was then that Jill looked at him seriously. "That's lovely, Mike, but not quite what I had in mind for our wedding. I was thinking more along the lines of maybe inviting my parents?" Her sarcastic tone put him off, and he sunk back into the couch.

"Don't be hurt. It will happen. And soon." She turned and brushed his hair back, although there seemed to be less of it these days, and added, "I love you, and I love that you want to do something so romantic. You've waited this long. Please hang on a few more months to plan the most beautiful wedding…"

"OOOOKAAAAAAY." Mike was not as good at being sarcastic. "You want a bottle of water?"

Jill nodded. "Thanks, honey."

As he pushed his way out of the couch, and walked away, a slight, Truman Capote-like figure approached Jill. "I really like your show. How did you meet Vee?"

"Oh, Hi!" Jill sat upright. "My fiancé, her saxophone player, Mike Munoz introduced us. And to whom do I have the pleasure?"

"My name is Randy Cole. I'm a producer." He spoke very matter-of-factly. "Mind if I sit down to talk?"

"Mike will be back in a second, if you don't mind him participating."

"Not a problem."

"How do you know Vee?" Jill wanted to be sure she wasn't getting herself involved with someone who might jeopardize her relationship and her contract with Vee, so she felt compelled to ask.

"Well, first, she's my cousin. Second, I produced her first and second albums." He smiled, and when he did, the tentative look he had when first approached disappeared. He no longer made Jill feel uncomfortable.

"Uh, does she know you're talking to me?

"She sent me over."

Just then, Mike returned juggling two bottles of water and a flimsy paper plate full of vegetables and dip, and some kind of salad he didn't recognize. "I sure wish Vee would get some kind of edible protein back here once in a while."

"Mike, this is Randy Cole." Randy stood and extended his hand, not to shake but to help Mike with his handful. He put the vegetable plate down and then reached out to greet him.

"Hi there, Mike. I was just getting to know your lovely, and talented, I might add, fiancé." Randy halted. "Hey, you're not the jealous type, are ya? Don't have to worry. See that guy over there talking to the bartender? That's my husband."

"Gotcha." Mike sat down on the couch. "So, what is it you were talking about."

"Well, my cousin Lila, or Vee as you know her, seems to think you are ready to cut an album, and she wants me to produce it. She also wants me to be the one to produce your first tour." Randy seemed to be laying out his agenda, as if it were a work assignment.

"Wait a minute." Jill was dumbfounded. "What are you talking about?"

"This happens every time. Vee wants you launched."

"What exactly does that mean?" Mike was not as overwhelmed, but curious.

"It means, according to your contract with her, you are done with tomorrow night's concert." He reached inside his jacket pocket and produced a copy of that contract. "As of Sunday, you are relieved of her employ. However, I am not."

Jill was confused. "You mean, you work for her?"

"I do. And you, my dear, are my next assignment."

* * * * *

"So, how's this idea. What if we call the album, 'Ear Candy?' You know, like eye candy is something great to look at, ear candy would be something great to listen to. I already have an idea for the cover." Randy spoke excitedly.

"I kind of like that." Jill was sprawled out on the couch at home, flashing her eyes back and forth across the ceiling trying to imagine what this guy was thinking of. "Tell me what you have in mind for the cover. It has to really go along with the branding I've been trying to achieve."

"Picture this… A totally white background, with a big jar of jelly beans. It will say Ear Candy across the top, and JayBee across the bottom, and the type will match a prominent color in the jelly bean jar."

Jill was astonished. "How did you come to Jelly Beans? Did Vee tell you about me and my name?"

Randy was surprised by Jill's aggressive reaction. "No, I just thought it was a clever idea. The back will have your picture, a bio, and song list, and for the inside, Vee is going to do an endorsement." He waited for some response. "Are you there?"

"I guess by the time the full CD is released, it will be okay. You never mentioned when the single is going live, by the way. You can't keep doing this to me."

"Jill, I have to do it this way. You get so worked up. I gotta keep you down, girl."

He's absolutely right.

"Okay, I need to go. I have to make a few personal calls and then I'll be in to work on some tracks for the last two songs." Jill sat up. "Randy, if I didn't say it enough, thank you for watching out for me."

"That's why they pay me the big bucks!" He hung up the phone.

* * * * *

"Daddio! How are you?" Jill called Arnie first. Mike suggested that get this whole thing moving and planned so she could finally be free of the angst. He promised her that the voices and the self-talking would calm down once the chaos she had created in her own life was taken care of.

"Well, hi there, Jelly Bean." Arnie hadn't spoken to his daughter in several weeks. He loved when she called in the mornings on the days when he didn't have surgery scheduled. His office appointments didn't start until ten and he had time to talk. "So, when exactly is the medical school graduation."

"It's in four weeks, and yes, there will be enough tickets!" The big reveal is scheduled for the night before, so she wouldn't need any tickets, but her Daddio didn't need to know that. "When are you coming up?

"It'll have to be the day before. We'll be checked in to the hotel in time for dinner. Will Mike be able to join us or will he be on tour again?" Arnie actually, liked Mike, especially now that he was making real money.

"He'll be there. He is on sabbatical for a few weeks. Someone else is filling in for him for the two weeks around my big event."

More lies, but not for much longer. Hang in there Jill.

"In fact, He wants to take everyone out to dinner Friday night. Are you okay with that?"

"I guess I'll have to be. It's not so easy getting used to the fact that I'm not the only man in your life anymore."

"Awww, Daddio! You will always have a special place in my heart. You were the first man I ever loved. Remember that!" She knew that would keep him happy for a little while, anyway. "I need to go catch the train. I'll talk to you soon. Give my love to mom and to the boys." Jill hung up the phone, feeling remorse, likely for the first time through this whole charade.

She dialed again. "Mike, now that it's coming down to the end, I have a horrible lump in my throat talking to my dad. I don't know if I'm going to be able to go through this. It's like for the first time, I actually feel the guilt about all of the lying."

"I have one thing to say to you, and I think you know what it is."

"Call my sponsor?"

"Yup."

"In a minute… as soon as we hang up. I want to tell you what he said first." She went on to give Mike the first part of the big plan. "They'll be here the Friday before, in time for dinner. I told him you wanted take everyone out. When you get home from rehearsal, we'll sit down and I'll explain how this is all going to work, okay?"

"Fine, baby. I have to tell you. I cannot wait until all of this is over. I don't know how it will end because I don't know your parents that well. I think you need to pray a lot, and leave the results in God's hands."

"Please, don't give me any program talk, okay. I'll call my sponsor, I promise. Love you." She pushed the little red receiver button on her cell phone before he could respond, and tossed the phone on the couch.

I'll think this through in the shower, and if I feel the need still, I'll call Shannon when I get out and dry off.

* * * * *

"So, what's your big plan for the great reveal?" Mike snuggled back into the couch cushion and crossed one leg over the other. He looked straight at Jill, his eyes penetrating. He had been ready for this moment for several years and he had high hopes that this woman, whom he had been supporting through all of the pretense, not because he wanted to, but because he had to, was going to finally begin to live her life with integrity and authenticity. He couldn't wait. "What, when, who, where, how… come on… I have to hear this."

Jill had spent the afternoon putting together an elaborate plan, but suddenly she had no confidence in it. "Mike, you're scaring me." She sat down on the edge of couch at his feet. "I need you to help me, not pressure me."

"Haven't I helped you all along? I may have sacrificed any respect I'll ever get from your Dad by doing so, too."

Jill looked down at her feet. She was, indeed, scared. She was also amazed that she had been able

to keep the whole thing going for almost eight years. There had been some close calls and she had to think on her feet a lot, but ultimately, she believed she had gotten away with it all.

"I know, Mike. I will make sure they know it was all me. I promise."

She took her time and then finally laid before him her scheme. "My folks are due in town in a couple of weeks, supposedly to attend my graduation from medical school, right?"

Mike nodded.

"They arrive on Friday, and the graduation ceremony isn't scheduled until Saturday afternoon, right?"

Again, Mike nodded. He was impatient, usually, but she could tell he was trying to give her time to map out the idea.

"So, where we go for dinner on Friday night is the key. Here's what I thought we could do. We take them to that Bar and Grill you like uptown… you know, the one that has karaoke on Fridays, and open mike on Sundays?"

"Yeah, I remember the one… its run by that older guy who plays folk guitar on Saturday nights." Mike started to sit up. Jill could tell his wheels were in motion. He started to say something but she interrupted.

"Hear me out. We all go and have dinner. When the karaoke starts, I'll drag Dad up to do a duet with me, right?"

"Yeah… I think I see where you're going with this."

"Wait. Let me finish. After we're done, I'm going to do a solo. I'll have them play "I Can Hear Your Heart Beat." But I'll turn my back to the crowd when I start singing. They'll recognize the voice. They'll have to." Jill was getting excited. "Then, I'll whip off my wig to expose my hair, turn around, and rock out…" She stopped talking and watched Mike intently. He was totally lost in the scenario.

"I love it. That just might work."

"But wait… then you hand my dad a letter, heartfelt, from me, explaining everything, with a check for some huge amount to pay him back for the medical school money he thought he laid out…"

Mike shook his head softly. "That might be too much for him to take all at once. You can take care of the money later. The letter is a good idea, though."

"Maybe you're right." Jill leaned in to kiss Mike. "It's all going to be over soon."

She climbed up next to him and snuggled in to the crook of his arm, resting her head in her favorite place, listening to his heart beat.

Chapter 21

The longest four weeks of her life were almost over and Jill felt more and more angst and anxiety as Friday drew near. She and Mike had been at Woody's Bar and Grill for dinner the week before on Friday night, just to be sure they still had karaoke, and more importantly, they had a song Jill could do with her dad. She also made sure her number one hit was available on the machine.

Her album had gone live three short weeks ago, "I Can Hear your Heart Beat" had been downloaded over one million times already, and it's up to number six on the billboard charts. She was ready to release the second single from the album and her tour would be on the road in one month. Randy has been working his tail off promoting her.

I have to go back to that mundane life I once lived for one more night and it starts tomorrow. Then, whether Daddio and mom like it or not, JayBee will follow her own bliss and Dr. Jill Kelly will be buried in their imaginations.

Jill sat down in the back of the room of the NA meeting, with the idea that a meeting before the upcoming weekend wouldn't hurt. Shannon was there. In fact, she was leading the meeting. Jill felt a lot of gratitude, having Shannon in her life.

She loved Mike, Vee and everyone else who has made her career possible, but without being clean and sober, none of it would have been possible. Shannon held her feet to the fire working steps and going to meetings, and even tolerated the fact that she was living this lie, knowing that it had a time limit.

* * * * *

"… Just remember… recovery is like eating an elephant. You have to do it one bite at a time." Shannon wrapped up the meeting, and then motioned for Jill to wait for her. She waded through the upsurge of people as they stood and stretched. "Hold on for a sec. I want to talk a few minutes before you go."

Jill stood by the coffee bar and waited. Shannon eventually got to the back of the room. Being clean for twenty eight years, you make a lot of friends in the program, so she had many people wanting her ear along the way.

"What's up?" Jill was expecting the usual.

"I just wanted to wish you good luck tomorrow night. Remember to breathe. It will all work out just the way it is supposed to.

Whatever their reaction is, you have to accept it, whether you like it or not."

"You know what? It never dawned on me that there would be anything other than a positive reaction. I mean, look at what I've accomplished?" Jill seemed baffled.

"Did you listen to what you just said?" Shannon had her sponsor face on. "You sound exactly like you did when I first met you. Look young lady, you made some very bad choices, continually lied to a very loving family, were completely overwhelmed by the guilt, therefore succumbing to addiction…" Shannon could have continued; however, she could see by Jill's facial expression, one of panic, that she may have pushed too far.

"I did, didn't I?" Jill hung her head. "So, if they're angry and hurt, it's because of my actions, and I have to accept whatever their reaction might be. That's what you're saying."

"That's exactly right. You may have made them very proud, or you may have alienated them forever. Somehow, I think it's going to be somewhere in between, but we don't know what we don't know. We'll take it one day at a time, okay. And remember, I'm here if you need me."

Jill threw her arms around her sponsor, and whispered in her ear, "Thank you so much. You hold me up and help me to see the things I look right past."

"Yeah, that's why they pay me the big bucks."

* * * * *

"Mike, do you think I should go get a fake lab coat?"

"Really Jill, at this point, are you really going to keep the farce so prominently in your own head as to go spend time and money to go do something like that?" Mike was tying his tie in front of the mirror in the bathroom.

"Why are you putting on a tie, anyway?"

"I just thought it would be a nice touch. After all, I'm taking my future in-laws out to dinner tonight!" Mike turned and smiled. "Now help me with this damn thing."

"You're a nut." Jill stood behind him while he squatted down to her height.

She only knew how to tie a tie if it was around her own neck so if he stood in front of her like that she could tie it directly around his neck. "Think I'll put on my blue dress. It always looks so cool with my hair. I mean once I take the wig off. I'm getting psyched."

"Me, too. Can I stand up, you're killing my back." Mike writhed to a standing position and tightened the tie himself. "Why don't you see if their flight landed on time. We should be hearing from them any minute."

"Could you do it? I want to get dressed." Jill's voice trailed off as she ventured into the closet.

Mike sighed. "The things I do…" He sat down on the bed and picked up his phone, punching at it until the airline website came up. "Did they fly into Kennedy or LaGuardia?"

"Kennedy."

"They landed about an hour ago. They should be at the hotel any minute." Mike shut down the website and then scanned his contact list for the hotel phone number. "They're at the Midtown Marriott, right?"

"Yeah, that's where dad always stays. He didn't say otherwise." She stopped rifling through the hangers. "What if he pulls a fast one and stays closer to the med school or something?"

"Don't worry. Nothing's going to happen. He's going to know the truth in just a few more hours."

* * * * *

Jill threw her arms around Arnie's neck and held him tight. When she released, she turned to her mother and did the same. Doris held her tight in return. "You okay sweetie?"

"Sure mom, just glad to see you." Then it was Eric's turn. Eric took the lead and wrapped his arms around her in a big bear hug.

"You look terrific, sis." He whispered in her ear, "So tonight's the night!" When he let her go, he winked at her, sending a wave of comfort through her.

If nothing else, Eric won't abandon me.

Ivan waved at Mike, not offering his hand to shake, confirming to Jill that there was no love lost there. Ivan had made it clear to her when she was home last that he felt she was making a serious mistake marrying a musician. At the time, she had laughed inside, but at that moment, she wondered how he was going to respond to this truth.

Mike spoke up. "The reservation is at eight. The hotel will take us in their hospitality van and I've instructed them to pick us up at eleven. That way we can relax and enjoy the evening." As he finished his sentence, the Marriott van pulled up in front of the doors.

* * * * *

Woody's was mobbed. Mike went in ahead of the Kelly family and looked for the owner. Woody Lane was an older guy, but a throwback to the sixties. A lot of his customers tease him about being a hippie who never grew up. His hair was graying, and long, and he wore it pulled back in a loose ponytail. His jeans were tattered, but clean, and he wore a T-shirt with a faded image of the photo from James Taylor's album cover of Sweet Baby James.

Woody was standing by the hostess podium reviewing the reservations when Mike approached him. "Evening Mr. Lane."

Mike always showed respect to Woody, having been given early opportunities to sit in with him during his early days in New York.

"Enough with the Mister stuff, Mikey. You're big time now. Call me Woody.

You got your whole party?" Woody was genuinely happy to see Mike.

"They're all just coming in now. Remember what I asked for, right?" Mike could hardly contain his excitement. "You have the Peter Paul and Mary song followed by JayBee's song lined up to open the karaoke portion of the show tonight, right?"

"Absolutely, and I have a big fat table, front and center, set for six." Woody pointed to the front of the restaurant, although it was difficult to see as all of the other tables were full and the bar along the far side was two and three people thick. "I sure hope your surprise is as big as you promised. I am giving away the farm tonight."

"Trust me, Mr. Lane. You won't be disappointed." Mike looked past Woody and saw his group in the lobby, and motioned them in. "Come by and meet everyone, would you please?"

"If I get a chance, sure." Woody was off toward the kitchen.

The Kelly's all filed in and followed Mike, meandering through the tables down to the front. Jill was bringing up the rear. The noise in the restaurant was deafening, enough to drown out the pulsing in her chest and head. She was perspiring profusely, and breathing fast, short breaths. When everyone was seated, she asked her Dad to switch with her so that he was facing the stage straight away. That put her on the other side of her mother, across from Mike, but next to Eric. She could seek comfort in Mike's eyes and Eric's very presence.

The hostess dropped menus at each place, and asked if she could take drink orders. Everyone passed except for Eric, Ivan and Doris. The boys had developed a taste for Kentucky bourbon, and Doris enjoyed a little red wine with dinner.

"So, Bean, you're not drinking so you'll have your head about you when you receive you M. D. degree tomorrow afternoon, heh?" Arnie was beaming. He had his whole family around one table again.

His entire outlook had changed since DeeGee passed, and Jill could see that he was genuinely happy. She decided to go along with it and stick to the plan.

"I guess. So, Ivan, I hear you made manager a few months back. That's terrific. And Eric, how's the internship going?" Jill tried quickly to change the focus. This was easy because Ivan loved to talk about himself.

"Geez, Jill. That was almost a year ago. Where have you been? Traveling around the world?"

What? Does he know something? He said world, right? Not country. Nah, he doesn't know. Eric would not have betrayed me.

"Sorry bud, it's been a long time since we've spent any time together." The server arrived just in time to save her, placing cocktails and water glasses around the table.

"Do you need any more time or are you ready to order? Woody's specials tonight is on the board in the corner over there." She motioned to the right of the stage. "Eighty-six the crab claws. They came in questionable, and Woody won't take the chance."

After everyone's order was placed, Arnie lifted his water glass to make a toast. "To my Jilly Bean and her successful completion of medical school. May her career bring her satisfaction and may her life with Mike bring her lots of Doctors and Musicians."

"DAD!" Jill overplayed her reaction as she knew he wanted her to.

"Have you set a date yet, kids?" Doris asked quietly. Nobody really heard her because of all of the ambient noise, but everyone knew what she asked. "I'd love to get to work on my only daughter's wedding."

Mike chimed in this time. "I've been trying to pin her down, Mrs. Kelly, but you know how it is. We promise you will be the first to know."

Just then, the room was silenced by the squeal of microphone feedback as Woody had climbed up on stage. "Yo, everyone! How are we doing tonight?"

Cheers and clapping. Whistling and floor thumping.

"Rowdy tonight, aren't we?" Woody removed the old microphone from its stand. "Glad you joined us tonight.

We're going to give you a little more time to eat, drink and enjoy, and then we have some big surprises for you tonight. So, dig in, and don't forget to tip your servers because I don't pay them much."

"Boooooo. Come on Woody." Clapping, Laughing, Whistling, Cheers.

Arnie stared at Woody as he climbed down from the stage. "They sure like this guy here."

He kept staring. "He looks so familiar to me, for some reason."

"He's Woody. Woody Lane. He owns the place." Mike answered the question. "He was an old folk musician, but ended up getting into the restaurant business. He always says it's because it guarantees him a gig on Saturday nights."

Arnie rested his chin in his left hand, with his elbow on the table, just watching. Doris hated bad table manners, so she knocked his arm off the table with the heel of her bread knife, bringing her husband back to the present.

It took two servers and two trays to deliver the food to the Kelly party.

Once everyone was served, the conversation died down all around the restaurant.

The din had changed from mumbling voices and clinking glasses to the clacking of silverware and murmurs of delight.

"I think your friend Woody made a good choice," Arnie said as he put another forkful of steak into his mouth.

* * * * *

At exactly nine o'clock, the lights dimmed. Servers frantically skittered around the room attempting to fill water and wine glasses, and coffee cups, while managing to clear away the dirty dishes.

"Now you see why I don't pay them very much. They're very noisy." Woody laughed a hearty laugh directly into the microphone. "Did you all enjoy dinner?"

Again, the clinking and clacking, the cheering and foot thumping started. This crowd was ready for some fun.

"Okay, then let's get down to business. If you haven't signed up to sing karaoke, and you've had enough to drink to wash away your inhibitions, there are still a few spots left. Go see my boy Perry in the corner over by the sound board." Woody paused to allow the sliding of any chairs. "My name, if you don't know by now, is Woody Lane. Welcome to Woody's Bar and Grill. Tonight, is karaoke night if you haven't figured that out yet. Perry… let me see the first part of the list now…"

Woody stepped over to the side and Perry handed him a small piece of paper.

"Ladies and gentlemen, give it up for Judy, singing Melissa Manchester's Midnight Blue."

The music started as a middle-aged, heavy-set woman walked out on stage, leaned in and gave Woody a kiss. She cleared her throat, looked at the lights, and whispered into the mike, "sorry Melissa…" With a raspy voice she began to sing.

Perfect tone, but no wind. She must be a smoker.

Jill's tendency to judge others had actually waned. After all, this was karaoke at an out-of-the-way bar and grill. She had learned to appreciate everyone and everything for whom or what they were.

Suddenly, Woody appeared behind Jill at the table. Mike whispered across the table to everyone the best he could without disturbing the singer. "Everyone, this is Woody. He gave me my first shot here in New York. Woody… the Kelly family. Arnie and Doris, Ivan, Eric, and the love of my life, Jill."

Woody bent over. He wasn't a good whisperer, but he tried. "Let's talk after the show. Pleasure to have you. I gotta get back up there." As fast as he appeared, he was gone.

* * * * *

"Oh, look at this. I just met these nice people. Will Arnie and Jill Kelly come on up and regale us with Peter Paul and Mary's version of Blowing in the Wind." Arnie looked at Jill with surprise. Clearly, he wasn't expecting this.

"Oh, come on, Dad. It'll be fun. I asked Mike to sign us up for a song I knew we could do, with a little harmony." Jill pleaded with him. When he hesitated, the rest of his family began cajoling him as well.

Arnie slowly slid his chair back, and the audience went wild, as if he were the original artist, himself. He made his way to the side of the stage and climbed the stairs. Woody met him at the side of stage and whispered something in his ear. Arnie stopped and looked at him intently and broke into a big grin, shook his hand and then joined Jill on stage.

She handed him the mike and the music began.

Jill's heart was hammering in her chest, but as they sang, Arnie reached for her hand and smiled at her. She dropped her shoulders and let him sing the second verse alone.

When the chorus came up the second time, she chimed in with harmony, the exact same way they used to sing it at the church parties. The crowd grew quiet as they sensed the complementary style in which they sang. During the last chorus, they invited the audience to participate. Voices fused together. Jill thought she saw people swaying lighters and candles back and forth in the rear of the room. When the last notes died out, Jill and Arnie, in synchronicity, dropped their heads and crossed the arms holding the mikes across their waists, as always.

The audience cheered for a few minutes.

Woody took his time returning to the stage. He took the mike from Arnie, and nearly yelled into it, "Jill and Arnie Kelly. Let's keep it going."

Arnie turned to leave the stage. Jill remained. She turned around and walked to the rear of the stage and stood silently while the clapping died down. Woody then put the mike back to his face. "Jill has agreed to stay and sing another. This one is for you young whipper snappers. She's going to sing JayBee's new number one single, 'I Can Hear Your Heart Beat.'"

Arnie had reached his seat and picked up his water to take a sip. He looked up at the stage to watch his little girl. Just as it did on tour, a spotlight began following Jill from above. The drums started a slow steady beat, a familiar one. Bum bum Bum bum Bum bum….

"I can hear your heart beat… I can feel your heart feel."

"Hey! That really is JayBee! I know that voice anywhere," came a scream from the crowd.

Suddenly, Jill reached behind her neck, got a hold of her wig and whipped off forward over her face, revealing her carrot top orange hair. She just kept singing. "I can know your thoughts as if we were one…"

People started rushing the stage. There were three or four rows thick of young people lined up in front of Jill as she sang and danced across the stage. "I can hear your heart beat… I can feel your heart feel."

They were singing right along with her.

Mike watched Arnie intently, waiting for the right moment to hand him Jill's letter. He decided better sooner than later so he pulled the envelope out of his pocket and slid it across the table.

"Arnie… here… Jill wanted you to see this."

"Not now." Arnie was mesmerized. He put his hand on top of the envelope and stared at the stage. Eric sat two seats away, watching both his father and his sister, trying to figure out how the whole thing would play out. Arnie, without thinking, had started tapping two of his fingers on the table in time with the music.

Jill was totally lost in the song, enjoying the fans at the front of stage, and hoping against hope that their reaction to her would help her cause.

As she reached that last very difficult line, her eyes met her father's. Because of the lighting, she couldn't quite make out his expression, but she put every ounce of energy into holding that last note. Like she did with her Daddio, when the song was over, she dropped her head, crossed her arm across her waist and took a bow.

Wonder if that was my last!

The glasses that hung over the bar were clanging from the thunderous roar of the audience. There were only three hundred and twenty people in the restaurant, which was its maximum, but it could well have been the Gardens as far as Jill was concerned. She felt as though the weight of the world had been lifted from her shoulders.

Now, they know.

When she left the stage, she did not come out front. She stayed back stage to avoid the audience.

If Arnie had read the letter, he would be back there any second. She waited. No Arnie.

Uh Oh. He's not coming. He's angry. Oh well. Shannon, where are you when I need you.

Do I go out there looking for him? Did I shock him too much? Is he okay?

Jill gathered her nerve and peeked out the side curtain, but she couldn't see Arnie anywhere.

Woody had Perry play some cover music for a few minutes, but she couldn't see Woody or her father.

What have I done? Where's Mike? Was he still at the table?

She looked out again, but the only ones still sitting at the table were Ivan, Eric and her mom.

They seemed to be happy, and smiling. Eric looked as though he was talking, probably explaining everything, I hop

Epilogue

"Settle down, settle down."   Woody stood at the microphone, begging for some order. People were milling around as if waiting for the announcement of the big winner in a contest or a raffle prize. "Please take your seats. Hey, I'm as surprised as you are. But I told you to expect something big. Was I right? Huh? Was I right?"

The crowd erupted again. Jill found a corner in the back, still waiting for her father but he was nowhere to be found. One of the servers brought her a glass of water, and stood while she sipped, making Jill very uncomfortable.

Was she trying to get the nerve to ask for an autograph?

She handed Jill a piece of paper. Jill glanced around one more time, handed the glass back and said, "I'm sorry, I'm just not up to it tonight."   The server looked confused, but walked away.

She continued to listen to what was going on out in the restaurant but as each minute passed, she began to feel emptier inside.

I've ruined everything for my father and for me. Is this really what I wanted?

"Guys, I'd like to introduce an old buddy of mine. A long time ago… seems like another lifetime… I was studying down at the University of North Carolina. See, I was going to be a doctor." He laughed into the mike again.

Jill sat up straight.

"I'd like to introduce you to my roommate from those days. Ladies and Gentlemen, Deke Kelly." Out from behind the far side curtain stepped Dr. Arnold Kelly, carrying a beat up old Gibson. "See, Deke and I used to play together… that's how we worked our way through school. We were known as Paradox Lost. Get it? Pair of Docs? Heh heh… Only I was the one that was lost. Deke went on to become one of the country's most innovative cardiologists, and well… you all know what happened to me."

By now Jill had read the note and was standing at the side of the stage watching in amazement as her father and Woody sat down on stools, side by side, and launched into that song… "Let Your Heart be Free."

With each measure, Jill stepped out closer and closer to the duo. She reached center stage, stood in behind them and began to sing, tentatively at first.

Arnie turned to her, smiled, nodded, and mouthed the words… Let your heart be free. I love you, Ms. Kelly.

Dear Daddio:

I really didn't know any other way to tell you this. I'm hoping you'll understand. It was you who taught me to stand up for what I want… You know, you 'gotta have heart.'

If you're not too angry, please meet me backstage.

Love,
Jelly Bean (JayBee)

Dear Bean (JayBee),

I have to say I'm a little disappointed that you lied to us, and that you're not going to be a doctor, but then, I always knew you were a special talent.

Don't worry; but we have a lot of talking to do. If you want to, please join Woody and me on stage and sing with Paradox Lost   for real.

Love,
Daddio (Deke Kelly)

ABOUT THE AUTHOR

J T Fisher writes for people who have a hard time talking about what's on their minds. Every book she writes introduces the reader into serious concepts but in a lighter, fictional way. Most people think about ending it all at least once in their lives. Judy is glad she didn't.

Her writing began as an empty nester blog to fill the time that was previously spent tending to her husband and two children. As she wrote and gained followers, she decided to try pure fiction. Judy felt that a lot of women, especially of her generation, struggled with many fears, questions, and issues growing up in the 1960s and 1970s, and many still carry those fears coupled with the shame, embarrassment, and skeletons that affect the way they live their lives even today. With two grown children, she now resides in Central Florida with one four-legged child named Mitzi and her husband. She enjoys reading, writing, live theater, and playing with her granddaughter, Amelia..